D1569352

THE ROOT CAUSE
ANGELICA R. ROBERTS

Paperback ISBN: 978-1-63616-135-8
eBook ISBN: 978-1-63616-136-5

Published by Opportune Independent Publishing Company

Printed in the United States of America

For permission requests, write to the publisher, addressed
"Attention: Permissions Coordinator" to the address below.
info@opportunepublishing.com
www. opportunepublishing.com

DEDICATION

To my Uncle P –
For your joy has spread,
Laughter remains,
And your approach to life has become my
blueprint.
Your influence and spirit lives on.
I love you.

Always,

Angelica

ACKNOWLEDGMENTS

I would first like to give thanks to God, who gifted me with the talent, love and desire to write. Thank you to my family and friends who continue to share in my appreciation and thirst for a pen and paper. Your support and encouragement means so much.

Special thanks to my test readers, Aneisha Hughes and Cam Bentley, for taking the time to read my early drafts, and providing me with excellent commentary that helped me sharpen the elements of the story. To my book consultants, Nova Roberts, Adrian Ackles and Quinton Roberts, thank you for your insight and input as I crafted exciting scenes and developed complex characters. I enjoyed digging deep and thinking outside the box with you. To Kristen Holloway, news anchor extraordinaire, thank you for shooting the book trailer and for taking part in the marketing process.

Thank you to my graphic designer, Helen Ackles, for designing a beautiful cover that brilliantly brings the novel to life. To my editor, Anita Bunkley, thank you for refining my manuscript and for offering me your expertise and excellent direction. Thanks to all of the Opportune Publishing staff, headed by Shanley Simpson, for your professionalism and personal touch.

Last but certainly not least, I would like to thank all of my readers for supporting my work! Please keep in touch by submitting reviews, leaving comments and sharing emails.

PROLOGUE

It was *Take Your Child to Work Day*. The glass door slid open, revealing an airy space of minimal décor that reeked of class and elegance. Conversation seemed to stop as the tall figure, led by beefy security and company personnel, entered the room. His presence alone demanded attention and respect from everyone present. Flanked on either side of this dominating man were smaller versions of him, shorter in size and much younger in age. For a second, the gentleman stopped to survey the room. He shared a quick smile, prompting his mini-mes to pause and revel at the picture before them. The building, situated prominently in the heart of Montgomery County, Maryland, just thirty minutes outside of the nation's capital, was a sight for sore eyes. The gentle splashes from the centrally placed waterfall provided a soothing feeling that created a calmness throughout the foyer.

Placing his Italian leather briefcase on the ground, the commanding man clasped his hands together in front of his body before delivering a deep baritone greeting to his employees. Managing a staff of more than 20,000, Thaddeus Simmons was Founder, C.E.O. and President of Simmons Enterprises, the largest black-owned arms, defense, information security and technology corporation in the United States. Considered a major contractor for the federal government, Thaddeus and his team of engineers raked in an average of $10 billion a year, a number that was only growing.

While Thaddeus greeted the room, his sons stood proudly by his side marveling at all that their father had created, and what they would one day acquire. At the young ages of thirteen and sixteen, they were familiar with this building and the effect that Thaddeus had on everyone he worked with and encountered. Donning matching double-breasted custom-made suits, as their father wore, Devin and Julian, stood silently waiting for Thaddeus to complete his good morning speech. Greetings floated in their direction, and before long, a young assistant rushed to retrieve the businessman's bag, holding a list of action items in her hand outlining the day.

Marching proudly to the elevator, the group headed to the top floor where a massive office overlooked the city. The boys stepped off the lift, pausing to look out of a window and take in the view. They could see all the way to the highway where traffic was backed up with cars and taxi cabs trying mercilessly to get to their destinations.

"Come on, boys," their father commanded.

Peeling their eyes from the street below, they followed Thaddeus and his assistant into the office space, with two different things on their minds. *Take Your Child to Work Day* was one of the boys' favorite days of the year and they each had different reasons why. For Devin, the older of the two, it reminded him that one day *he* would be in the big seat, heading the major corporation. A fact he didn't take lightly. For Julian, the youngest, it meant seeing all the fine honeys his dad employed around the office. Julian was always more infatuated with the beautiful assistants that his dad kept around than he was, the company.

Each boy carried certain characteristics of their dad. One was a workaholic and the other was a self-proclaimed ladies' man. It was no secret that Thaddeus, who'd been married for almost eighteen years to the boys' mother, worked hard but played harder. In fact, the shapely assistant who swayed her hips as she guided the three of them into the office was his latest assistant, or one might call her his latest mistress, known as Tara. Tara was barely twenty years old. Both Julian and his daddy couldn't stop salivating over her.

Catching his brother's not-so-subtle glances toward the young woman, Devin hit him in the back of the head to get his attention off of their father's new office flavor's ass.

"Damn, man! What's wrong with you?" he howled, touching the sore spot where Devin had hit him.

Before Julian could carry on against his brother, Thaddeus, who'd heard the cuss word and ruckus, turned around, shooting a look that made Julian quickly shut his mouth.

Entering the room, the small group noticed two gentlemen sitting on the leather chairs facing the desk.

"Uncle Jacob!" Julian called out in excitement before sending a quiet nod of acknowledgment to the other man in the room.

"Hey, Mister Regis," Devin offered.

Jacob Grayson stood up to greet the boys he called his *nephews*.

Looking on from his chair, Regis Adams simply grunted.

A long-time-friend of the boys' father, Jacob was Chief Operating Officer of Simmons Enterprises, and a permanent fixture in their lives. Regis Adams, was a newer friend of his, and low on the list of people the boys enjoyed being around. He was stern and dismissive of them, unlike Jacob, who was warm and fun.

Thaddeus and Jacob shared a lifelong friendship, which stemmed from their days as plebes at the Naval Academy in Annapolis. After meeting during the first week of their freshman year, the two became inseparable. Thaddeus was the charming brainiac who came from a decent middle-class family in Atlanta, while Jacob, a native of Maryland, was the swift talker who made it out of his rough neighborhood and into the prestigious military college partly due to his can-do, 'don't take no for an answer' attitude. He always seemed to be able to talk his way in or out of anything and had a talent for getting out of sticky situations.

After serving his time in the military, Thaddeus decided to build his own business and brought his trusted friend with him. Together they went from meeting in a shabby office space where the heat never seemed to work in the winter, to owning and operating a multibillion-dollar business. Their story had been covered in *Black Enterprise, Forbes* and *Fortune,* and was always interesting to read about.

Fist bumping both of the young boys, Jacob then turned to Thaddeus with a smile.

Regis quietly observed.

"Whatsup, Thad?"

Sending a nod in Jacob's direction, and a silent look to Regis, Thaddeus took a seat behind his massive desk, wondering why Regis had randomly popped up in his office.

The boys took a minute to look around their dad's office. It seemed to always change each time the duo visited, and usually signaled that their dad had invited a new mistress into his life. Thaddeus always liked to make his women feel special by proposing intimate projects for them to work on. Artwork that once adorned the walls, compliments of the previous mistress, had been replaced by authentic African pieces in glass cases spread throughout the room. Devin was almost positive that it was all Tara's handiwork.

"Nice art, dad," Devin said.

In the corner stood Tara, smiling at the compliment as if it had been delivered to her. Preparing for his first meeting of the morning, Thaddeus instructed Tara to look after the two boys. She shuddered at the thought of having to babysit. Julian grinned from ear to ear at the idea of having her around for the whole morning.

"Thad, I'll meet you in the boardroom. I want to catch up with my nephews for a second," said Jacob, motioning for the boys to come over to him.

"That's perfect," Regis said. "Thad, I wanted to holler at you really quick before you get the day started."

Thaddeus bristled in response. The whole purpose behind the meeting that morning was to sit down with Jacob and discuss some personal concerns that were interfering with the business, not to have an impromptu meeting with Regis; but instead of responding, he gathered up his papers and readied himself to leave.

One quick glance to his phone made him stop in mid-motion. Something wasn't right. He'd missed four back-to-back calls from a contact of his in the FBI, with whom he had plans to meet with later that day. Concerned, he quickly stood up to hug his sons goodbye before heading out of the room. One would think his strong frame would crush the boys, but when it came to them he was a gentle giant.

It was then that Devin could sense something was wrong.

"I love you both," said Thaddeus quietly before releasing them. He walked to the door before turning around. "Give me like fifteen minutes, Regis, I have a call to return."

Regis gave a slight nod, and the group remained behind. It was obvious that something was off.

Thaddeus proceeded down the hall where he whipped out his phone to call his contact. Not even five minutes later, loud voices rang out throughout the building. FBI agents bulldozed their way into the corporate spaces, citing a search warrant for Simmons Enterprises.

Rushing from the office to check out the disturbance, everyone was shocked at the scene below. Downstairs, dozens of federal agents crowded the first floor, instructing members of the staff to step away from all company issued devices. The sounds of drawers being ripped out and papers tossed on the floors were loud and frightening. Employees scattered in every direction, afraid of what was happening, while the boys looked out through the glass window in horror.

As this was happening, Thaddeus, who'd just been briefed of this surprise search minutes prior by his contact on the inside, was directed to his private elevator by his chief of security.

Downstairs, the lead agent in charge turned to look at the growing crowd of spectators and demanded Thaddeus's location. No one dared to speak, partly because no one knew where he was. Clenching his hands into fists, the agent in charge faced his fellow officers and hollered, "Find him!" On his command, agents bounded up the stairs, heading to the top of the building, looking for the man they suspected of killing a United States Congressman. A government agent in a rush to get to the top floor, pushed past Devin on his way up, knocking him to the floor. He stopped briefly to check the young boy over, then helped him to his feet.

"Sorry kid," he muttered before hurrying off.

Running towards his helicopter on the roof of the 40-story building to head to his attorney's office in New York, Thaddeus shook with fear. He rarely used the small plane, but this was not a normal day, and his contact had instructed him to leave immediately. Still not sure what all was happening, he paused mid-stride for a few seconds to call his wife.

"Hello..."

"Brenda, I don't have time to talk but something is going on and I need to get out of here. You need to pick the boys up right now. Don't talk to anyone, just get the boys and go straight back home. I'll call you back with more details."

Brenda, who was barely awake at the start of the call, was now on full alert.

"But what the hell is going on—"

"Not now, baby. I love you, I'll call you back when I have more details."

Without waiting for her to respond Thaddeus hung up and continued on to the helipad. The sound of the chopper was thunderous, but for Thaddeus the world was quiet, as reality set in. Life as he knew it would never be the same. However, before he was able to board the small plane, a voice boomed in the distance.

"Thaddeus Simmons, step away from the helicopter."

Thaddeus, now surrounded by guns held by federal

agents, became dizzy at the sight of weapons pointed in his direction, and his world swirled out of focus. Unable to get his bearings, he stood frozen in place. At that moment, his phone rang. The tune that it played told him it was his oldest son, Devin. Knowing better than to reach into his pocket, Thaddeus turned around with his arms raised in surrender. Charging towards him, agents placed him in cuffs.

"Thaddeus Simmons, you're under arrest for the murder of Congressman Rucker. You have the right to remain silent, anything…"

The arresting officer continued, but Thaddeus could barely make out the words being recited to him. He felt like he was floating through time as he was led off of the roof and through the building, in front of his employees, and to his shame, his children.

Jacob held onto the boys as they tried to fight their way through the crowd, to get to their father. Before reaching the door with his head hung low, in the very place that he had not so long ago walked through with his head held high, Thaddeus turned to face his children, fear clouding his eyes, as he whispered, "I'm innocent."

Two months of sitting in a jail cell awaiting a trial date went by as Thaddeus spent time alone, brooding over how he'd gotten involved in this situation. The air was cold, and the conditions were grimy. The place reeked of death. Then one day, a correctional officer came to his cell.

"Simmons, come with me," said the stocky guard, as he cuffed him and led him out of the confined space.

The guard took him to the small room where he normally

met with his attorney. Thaddeus was agitated to see the one person who'd gotten him mixed up in this mess, seated with his legs crossed, wearing a smirk on his face.

Refusing to sit down, he eyed the intruder. The guard forced Thaddeus into the seat across from his guest before turning around to leave.

"What the fuck are you doing here?"

"Wow, wow, calm down, killer," laughed the unwelcome visitor. "I come in peace. Damn, it's only been a couple of months and this place has already done a number on you, man. Now you're starting to talk like the guys I grew up with in the hood instead of the preppy boy I've always known you to be. It's a shame you were denied bail."

Thaddeus stared at the man whom he had once thought was like family to him, annoyed to see his eyes dancing in excitement. Thaddeus thought about lunging at him over the steel table and knocking the self-righteous look off his face. Gripping his hands on the edge of the table to prevent himself from attacking his visitor, he knew the guards were looking on in case they needed to intervene.

Unbuttoning the top button of his dress shirt, his visitor got comfortable and let out another small laugh.

"I just wanted to come and see you in person. You're looking worse than you do on television. Life's been hard on you, man."

"No, you wanted to know if I dropped *your* name yet, that's why you're here. Well, no I haven't. You can leave now."

The visitor sat back and studied Thaddeus for a minute.

"It's a shame that you continue to lie to me, Thaddeus. I know you tried to sell me up the river. You didn't think I would find out?" Leaning forward in his chair, he lowered his voice so that only Thaddeus could hear.

"Well, now let me tell you what my plans are. I've been around your nappy headed boys and that grieving drunk wife of yours a lot these past few weeks. I will continue being around them, you know, just to give them a shoulder to lean on while you're in here. What do you think about that?"

Jumping up from his seat, Thaddeus banged on the table, causing his visitor to double over in laughter. The guards approached the men, ready to take their inmate back to lockup, but before they could, the visitor delivered a message.

"You forgot who I am, son. Forget about that damn family of yours, you should really watch your back in here. It would be a shame if you don't make it to see your trial date. Frankly, I'm surprised you even made it off of that roof alive."

Thaddeus looked at the guards, certain they had heard the threat. Surprisingly, they ignored it and ushered him out of the room.

Grinning as he watched Thaddeus being led back to his cell, the visitor picked up his phone to make a quick call.

On the first ring, the receiver answered.

"Kill him."

CHAPTER 1

THE ANNOUNCEMENT

The air conditioner, set to 64-degrees did nothing for the stately man perched on top of a stool facing the lens of a camera. Squirming on top of the small chair, Devin Simmons loosened his steel blue tie in hopes of cooling off. The room was spacious but the number of people crowding inside made him feel like he was trapped in a box. Beckoning for something to drink, his assistant approached with a bottle of Eleven86, and the camerawoman used the small break to further adjust her settings.

"You really need to loosen up," said Darlene McIntyre, who stood on the left side of the room.

Downing the water like it was a shot of tequila, her client merely grunted in response.

"Seriously, Devin, you only get one first impression, so you need to knock this out of the ballpark."

"Don't you think I know that?" he snapped.

Devin Simmons was a ball of nerves as he began to re-think his bid for a United States Senate seat in Maryland. Normally self-assured and confident, in that moment he began second-guessing himself, wondering if he could really pull it all off. His most serious competition, Senator Brennan, was running for re-election and was going to be a tough act to beat, but luckily there were two seats up for grabs and the other candidates were lesser known. At thirty-three, Devin was a wildcard. Though considerably younger than the other people in the race, in the past few years he had become well-known in political circles, gaining national attention for his efforts to increase voter registration and protect civil rights. Not only did he fight to have legislation passed prohibiting racial profiling at traffic stops, but he was also credited for the work he was doing on behalf of criminal justice reform, jobs, the economy, and veterans. Devin had been featured on several *People to Watch* lists, nominated for prestigious awards, and was admired by everyone he met. He was well poised, good looking and full of charm—a real shoo-in for Congress. Being a millennial added to his potential and he was certain to pull in younger voters. With aspirations of reaching the highest office in the land one day, he knew this race meant a lot. The state had never elected a black senator, let alone one so young, and there had only been eleven African American senators to serve in the U.S. Senate to date, a list that included former President Barack Obama and Vice-President Kamala Harris.

Darlene rolled her eyes and decided to keep her usually sharp tongue silent. A reputable political strategist who always got the job done, Darlene was used to working with the alpha types and had learned different ways of dealing with them throughout the years. This was her first take as a campaign manager, but she was confident in her ability to bring the team a win. Her time as a field organizer in the 2018 presidential campaign and field director for a major U.S. Senate campaign had prepared her, and she was ready to get Devin elected.

The door to the small studio flew open and a scent that could only be worn by one person seeped into the room. Darlene smiled at the beautiful woman who walked through the door. If anyone could get Devin to relax, it would be his fiancée, Vanessa Covington. Dressed in a brown wrap dress appropriate for the late winter weather and an oversized tan coat, her aura alone brought the small space alive, Devin included.

"Hello everyone," she greeted in her usual melodic voice.

Grateful for the distraction, Devin stood to embrace the beautiful woman who had the room at full attention, kissing her softly on the forehead. Her hands grazed his face, detecting droplets of sweat that had formed on his brow.

"Sorry I'm late, my hair appointment took longer than expected."

Fingering the curls that framed her petite face, Devin smiled for the first time that morning.

"You're right on time, and you look beautiful."

"You look hot," she said. "And not in a good way."

Placing her bag on a nearby table, Vanessa approached Devin and removed his tie. Once the material was off she instructed him to unfasten his top button. Never the one to step on anyone's toes, she looked back at Darlene for approval.

"Looks good to me," Darlene said. "Makes him look more easy-going and it'll appeal to the younger voters.

Good call, Vanessa."

Shooting his wife-to-be a grateful smile, Devin retreated back to the stool with newfound confidence. Clapping his massive hands, he donned the magnetic smile he'd become known for around the state, and said, "Let's make this happen."

Within five minutes the camera began rolling and a confident and much cooler Devin faced the lens to begin his announcement.

"Former Senator Carol Moseley Braun once said, 'Magic lies in challenging what seems impossible.' Currently, we are facing uncertain times and it is imperative that we have the right people in place to fight for the issues plaguing all Americans, like gun violence, equal rights, tax reform and health care. This is why I am excited to announce that today I am launching my campaign to be the next U.S. Senator for Maryland."

With one take, Devin had managed to deliver excitement, empathy towards causes closest to his heart, and confidence. Three things that would win the votes and trust of Maryland residents. The video, which would be played for days to come on every major network, media outlet and social media account, was the beginning of a tough race, but a great start.

The studio erupted in applause and his camp congratulated him on taking this leap of faith. They celebrated what was sure to be a long but successful journey to Congress.

"And just like that, the race begins people!" Darlene shouted.

While the staff stood around and talked, excited about

what was to come, Devin took off his suit jacket and took a moment to speak with the man who had already made an enormous contribution to his campaign. Regis Adams, a former friend and guide to Devin's late father had become somewhat of a mentor to Devin when he entered politics over a decade earlier. Grabbing him into a hug, the older man grinned at the thought of his late protégé's son becoming such a major force in the political arena.

"Devin, great job, that sounded wonderful."

"Thanks for coming to support, Regis."

"Come on now, you know I had to come and see where all my money was going," he said, grabbing Devin's shoulder with a laugh. Over the years, Regis had made millions of dollars through his investments and real estate deals and was a well-respected businessman.

Hearing the laughter caused Vanessa to turn away from the conversation she was having with a few of the campaign staffers and face the two men who were chatting. She noticed the adoring look on Devin's face as he spoke with the man he held in such high regard. While one of the staffers in front of her kept talking, she couldn't help but zone him out and think about how off-centered Regis always seemed to be. He was always nice and gracious, but there was something in his eyes she could never trust, even after two years of being around him. Plus, even though he had a wife whom he seemed to love, he gave off misogynistic vibes. Some of his comments never sat right with her.

Feeling a set of eyes on him, Regis looked up from his conversation with Devin and stared directly at Vanessa, making her squirm under his gaze.

Leaving a talking Devin in mid-sentence, he approached

Vanessa with arms outstretched and a wide grin.

"Vanessa, you're looking more beautiful than ever these days."

Reaching in for a hug, Vanessa returned an embrace and planted what she hoped looked like a genuine smile on her face.

"Hi, Regis, it's always great to see you."

"Are you ready to be First Lady? I know the people will love you. You'll be our next Michelle Obama."

The thought of amounting to even half the woman Michelle Obama was brought a real smile to her face. That was Regis, he always knew the perfect thing to say to people.

"That's a stretch, but I'll fit the role the best way I can."

"She's so humble and modest," Devin said, as he walked up. "People already love her. She'll do great."

The pair looked at each other for a second with puppy dog eyes, until Regis interrupted their moment.

"Well, I think it's time I leave the two of you to your day. Brenda told me she wanted to throw you a dinner to raise money for your campaign in a few weeks. I guess that'll be the next time we cross paths."

This was news to Devin, as his mother hadn't shared this information with him. Tensing up at the thought of her hosting something in his honor, he tightened his jaw.

"Come on, Devin, you know your mother means well. Anyway, I'll be seeing you soon."

The room slowly cleared out, and it was time for the real work to begin.

CHAPTER 2

ONE LAST HURRAH

On the top floor of 200 Street Paul Place in Baltimore, Ian Thompson sat on an uncomfortable chair inside a small office. A worn loose-leaf notebook filled with notes and ideas for potential stories was closed, on his lap. It was seven in the morning, a pinnacle time in the world of news. Opposite him stood Simon Roe, Managing Editor of the *The Daily Sun*, who paced back and forth behind his desk while he spoke. Noticeably nervous and intimidated by the man sitting before him, he could barely make eye contact. With a blank stare, Ian looked on as his editor, a man half his age, mumbled something about budget cuts and low readership.

For decades, Ian Thompson, had been one of the best journalists at the *The Daily Sun* and one of the most decorated. From his Pulitzer Prize award-winning article on the war on drugs, his book on his investigative reporting of El Chapo, to his role in uncovering government and corporate corruption and weekly commentator gigs with major television networks, the name Ian Thompson was mentioned around the world.

But even with all his accolades, he heard the whispers. It had been four years since his last big headline, and some were arguing that his juice had finally dried up. Glancing down at his unopened notebook, which contained ideas that he knew would be unimpressive, he felt certain that Simon, through all his nervousness, was about to officially can him.

For a moment he allowed himself to tune Simon out as his eyes caught a caption running across the screen of one of the small television sets mounted right outside the office:

I am excited to announce that today I am launching my campaign to be the next U.S. Senator for Maryland.

Following the short clip, the anchor appeared on screen with a statement that almost made Ian fall out of his seat: *Out of Maryland, Devin Simmons, son of the late disgraced businessman, Thaddeus Simmons, has announced his bid for a seat in the United States Senate.*

"Ian, are you still with me here?"

Simon had finally stopped pacing when he noticed that the reporter's attention was somewhere else. Gathering up his coat, which was strewn behind him on the chair, Ian didn't have time to wait for Simon to spit out whatever he had to say.

"Look Simon, I get it. You guys think I'm old and washed up. You want me to retire, right?"

Stunned at his forwardness, though he should have been used to it by now, Simon quickly opened his mouth to refute what Ian said.

Waving his hands, Ian stopped him. "No, it's okay.

Really. I think it's time for me to leave too, but..."

Looking back at the television screen and thinking about Thaddeus Simmons, a name that had haunted him for years, he knew his job wasn't yet complete.

"I have one more story in me."

CHAPTER 3

MORNING AFTER

A couple of days had passed since his big announcement and Devin was ready to get to work. Waking up with a start, the day was full of interviews and exclusives with magazines and news stations. The sun was peeking out from behind the clouds as Vanessa lay peacefully on her side of the bed. Snoring softly and oblivious to Devin shuffling around the room, she was the image of beauty. For a second, Devin stopped to admire the woman with whom he had made a commitment to spend the rest of his life. She was outwardly gorgeous, but it was her inner beauty and compassion for others that made him fall in love. The pair had met at a charity event for cancer in Arlington, Virginia two years prior and had been together ever since. They had connected on a level that was unlike anything either of them had ever experienced.

Following a speech dedicated to the life of her late

grandfather, a civil rights activist and humanitarian, Vanessa retreated to the backstage area and released a flood of tears. Her grandfather, Bishop Isaiah Barrett, had died earlier in the year, and she was still devastated. At eighty-two he had been in great shape, which was why everyone was confused and heartbroken when they learned he passed away in his sleep. Always vibrant and caring, the late Bishop Isaiah Barrett had participated in sit-ins for racial equality, organized community events, and had worked with the likes of Al Sharpton, Jesse Jackson and Maxine Waters to get the message out to the masses about hate crimes and racial injustice happening not only in the United States, but also around the world. He was a widely respected man in the south and internationally, but to Vanessa he was simply her Papa.

It was he, who taught her the importance of standing up for the things she believed in, and she ended up choosing the same path in life as his. After graduating with a degree in African American studies, Vanessa became a community leader and was active within several organizations dedicated to civil rights and the social liberties of everyone, just like her Papa. Closer to him than her father, who was more of a complainer than a doer, news of Papa's death hit her hard.

Tears streamed down her face, which was hidden underneath her hands, until a soft voice made her look up. Seeing the visible distress on her face, Devin, whom Vanessa had noticed from the event, had taken his handkerchief from his blazer pocket and handed it to her.

"Want to talk about it?" he asked gently.

In that moment, Devin felt the urge to draw a somber Vanessa into his arms, and he did just that. Grateful to have someone around to comfort her, she welcomed his strong arms around her body and nestled her head on his shoulder, taking in the subtle scent that was a mix of scotch and cologne. A few moments passed before Vanessa, reluctant to let go, lifted her head and stared into the eyes of the man who had given her a comfortable space.

It was then that she realized just how attractive he was. Devin had a boyish look that shaved a few years off of his age. The glasses he wore, mostly for fashion and not because he needed them, made him appear astute and present. He towered over her, which was no small feat seeing that she was five-foot-seven, and his athletic build told her that he worked hard for those chiseled arms, the ones that had just held her. Embarrassed at her meltdown, the granddaughter of the historical figure said a quick thank you before turning away to walk to the bathroom and freshen up.

"Wait," Devin said. Lightly grabbing her elbow and turning a blushing Vanessa back around, he was in awe of the woman standing in front of him. He had been mesmerized by her beauty when he'd heard her speaking during the event. Even from his table, located farther from the stage, he had noticed just how attractive she was. Up close, he considered her a classic beauty, rivaling the Nia Long's of the world. With her golden-brown complexion, bright smile and eyes that shone like diamonds, she quite literally took his breath away. Her hair was cut in a smart bob and the attention Devin was giving her made her run her fingers through it to make sure no strand was out of place. Then a sound came from the main room signaling the start of the jazz band.

"Dance with me later?" Devin asked.

Without any words, Vanessa gave him a small smile and nodded before turning around to head to the ladies' room. The rest of the night had been a blur as Devin sought her out in the crowd of attendees. They danced for what seemed like hours, laughing and talking as if they were old friends. After learning his name, Vanessa knew he was the same man whose father was once a mogul in the business world, but had since died. It was then that she realized what he meant by the words, *I know how it feels to lose a loved one*. He had been referring to his father. That night, the two knew they had found love and comfort in one another.

Now, sending a quick prayer of thanks to God, Devin continued his daily routine and headed for the shower. The bathroom was quickly blanketed by the steam coming from the hot water streaming out of the shower head. Lathering his body, focused on not missing any parts, a gust of wind blew past as Vanessa quietly entered the cloudy bathroom. Dropping her silk robe to the floor, she joined Devin inside the standing room only space, ready to help him start his morning off right.

Her soft fingers reached forward to take the washcloth from Devin's hands, and from behind him she slowly began moving the material up and down his body parts, exciting him with each subtle movement. The sound of moans began to fill the room. After making sure all the suds were off his body, Vanessa turned around to place her hands on the shower wall, while slightly bending her knees to make her sweet spot more accessible. Following her lead, Devin turned his back to the shower head and began massaging her breasts. Reaching down to meet her slender frame, he lowered his face and grazed her lips before bringing his hands down to meet her thighs. He kissed her inner thigh, showing love to the area where her beauty mark rested. Slowly moving his lips to her clit, a gasp escaped Vanessa, letting him know her body was ready for him to enter.

With one swift thrust, his pulsating member glided inside, causing her to moan louder. Always one to make sure his lady orgasmed first, a shaking Vanessa told him it was finally time for him to release too, and he did just that. After catching their breaths, they rinsed off and stepped out to towel each other off.

"Girl, do you know how much I love you?" he asked.

"You better," she replied, giddily.

They stood silently for a few moments, gazing at one another. They had a healthy sex life and enjoyed switching it up and having fun. They were open with one another about their sexual desires and preferences, and had moments of extreme kinkiness.

Before the campaign began, Vanessa had even suggested they bring additional partners into their bedroom. Knowing Devin would one day run for a major office, the couple discussed ways they could keep their potential sexual escapades private. Their plans were placed on hold when opposition research, organized by Darlene, revealed a number of private moments that could be used by Devin's opponents to discredit him and weaken his chances of winning. They stopped all talks of having multi-partners after that. Breaking their stare, Vanessa playfully pushed Devin back into the bedroom.

"Okay Senator, now finish getting ready to go out there

and make me proud."

Grinning, Devin walked to the walk-in closet to grab the suit his stylist had set aside for him to wear. Vanessa sat on the bed, watching him get ready.

"I heard Miss Ruby downstairs. I have a feeling she made all your favorites for breakfast. You know she won't let you leave this house without eating a full plate."

Nodding his head in agreement, he already knew the older woman wouldn't let him leave on an empty stomach. Putting on his tie as he looked into the mirror, he grabbed his phone and paused briefly to scroll through some of the texts. A groan escaped his mouth when he saw one text in particular filled with emojis and exclamation points:

Mom: *Hello my oldest son! I'm hosting a dinner for you in a couple weeks. Let me know what day works best with your schedule.*

Once he read the text aloud, Vanessa immediately knew why his eyebrows were wrinkled in frustration. Devin's mom was a hot mess and couldn't be trusted to host anything for him, especially during an election season. After her husband committed suicide while awaiting trial, Brenda Simmons strengthened her already familiar relationships with Gin, Vodka and Hennessy, and just about anything else she found at the local liquor stores or ordered through a food app. During the campaign she was intentionally left out of a slew of engagements and press conferences. Some days were better than others for her, but Devin couldn't take that chance and decidedly kept her behind closed doors.

Standing up to straighten his tie, Vanessa stood on her tippy toes to give Devin a reassuring kiss, and then ordered him downstairs before Ms. Ruby, his longtime housemaid who had become like family, came to get him.

"Go on down there before she comes to find you," she joked. "She'll blame me if you're late."

Devin knew she was trying to keep his mood positive, and appreciated her for trying.

"See you tonight, babe."

Just as he turned towards the door, he heard a shrill voice coming from downstairs.

"Devin get on down here! This omelet won't eat itself!"

Looking back at Vanessa, the pair cracked up, laughing.

"I'm coming, Ms. Ruby!"

CHAPTER 4

PRESS AND RELEASE

The days that followed were a whirlwind. Campaign donations were coming in fast and plentiful, and Devin had been dubbed by supporters as, *the chosen one*. Still amazed by the amount of support he was receiving, Devin became more and more excited about the prospect of representing his home state as time went on. Born in Maryland, Devin matriculated through grade school before choosing to attend college in the Chocolate City. Like Vanessa, he'd proudly attended a top ranked historically black college where he received his bachelor's degree in political science, then later returned home to earn his Juris Doctorate at the University of Maryland Francis King Carey School of Law.

In addition to his obvious intellect, Devin was pleasing to the eye. Standing tall, an even six-foot-three, he was what some would call a pretty boy. His chestnut skin was free of blemishes, minus a small scar that sat on his right cheek, the result of a motorcycle accident during his undergraduate years. His smile radiated throughout every room he walked into as he displayed two rows of perfectly aligned white teeth, thanks to the braces he'd worn during his puberty years. Though he had never been an athlete, he had an athletic build, and even his slightly bowed legs seemed to add to his appeal. Women and men took notice whenever he walked by, but unlike his younger brother, Julian, he only had eyes for one person, Vanessa.

Gearing up for his radio interview on Power 105.1, Devin sat in the building going over his talking points with Darlene, who was running point.

"This is going to be a great interview, Devin. Angela Yee personally contacted me and requested that you come on the show. Our demographic will be listening, and it's important we get everyone behind us, even those outside of Maryland. It helps that DJ Envy is an HBCU grad and advocates for them. It'll be a perfect fit."

Devin knew how important it was to be authentic and charismatic during the interview. The radio show hosts were known for smelling bullshit and would be asking the questions that voters would want to know the answers to, so the young candidate running for Congress had to be on his game. Without looking up from his notecards, Devin nodded and continued prepping.

Ninety minutes later, the show was recorded and the four of them stood in front of the Breakfast Club backdrop to pose for photos. Well wishes were given and Devin was sent on his way. Before he could even make it to his town car, his phone rang. Answering on the first ring, the voice on the other end was animated and loud.

"Mr. Simmons, after that interview your name is all over social media! You're trending and people are even talking about those sweaty workout videos you do. They're calling you the Sexy Senator," laughed the young girl on the other end of the line.

Devin was a health nut who worked out at least five times a week. He'd started posting his workouts at the urging of Darlene. She thought it would be appealing to voters. He felt like a piece of meat with each *like* he received, but it was working. His following doubled in a month once he added that content to his personal page. Darlene also thought it was important that they have a diverse group of people in age and race on their campaign team, and had appointed Shelby, who was in her freshman year of college, to handle his social media.

Pulling the phone back from his ear at her screeching laugh, Shelby kept talking, unaware of how high her voice was.

"Yeah, I just wish they didn't mention that stuff about your father being accused of all those crimes, then killing himself before the trial and all, but I think you answered their questions well. You did a good job reminding the people about your position on white collar crime and prison reform, and that you're your own man. Great way to tackle that one."

Devin grimaced at the thought of that question. Questions about his father always put him in a weird place, but his media training taught him how to deal with them.

"Oh, and they're talking about that clap-back you gave when 'Tha God' asked how you handle questions about your sexuality, and you said—the same way you handle them. That was iconic! Then, he pointed out how you've done a good job keeping the focus on the issues and not your private life. It's actually pretty great to see you, an openly bisexual candidate, being taken seriously. You're opening up so many doors just by running."

Devin had never wanted to be the poster boy for a movement, but he knew exactly what Shelby meant, and was happy he'd taken advice from his old friend, Maya, when it came to discussing his sexuality.

"Well, sir, I have to go now, I have to respond to some of these tweets. Great talking to you!"

And just as quickly as she had arrived, she was gone. Jumping into the car next to Darlene, Devin looked out the window to take in the hustle and bustle of the Big Apple. As the town car passed by the thousands of people walking the busy streets, Shelby's comments sent him back to the day when he'd finally come to terms with his sexuality. Sitting quietly, he thought back to a few years earlier, when he reconnected with his childhood friend, Maya Kincaid.

Pulling into a spot farthest from the entrance to the church, Devin's heart had felt like it was beating out of his chest as he looked around the parking lot. He was an hour early and cars were slowly pulling in behind him, but he was in no rush to leave the safety of his SUV. Facing the woman whom he had been disloyal to ten years earlier almost made him turn the car around. The engine softly hummed in the background as Devin dabbed the sweat on his forehead with his handkerchief and wondered silently if it was a good idea to attend the wedding of his childhood friend, Maya. Even though they'd grown up together, with their families being close friends, a lot had changed since they were young. Questions raced through his head, but the biggest one was, *has she forgiven me*?

Maya Kincaid had invited Devin to her wedding, which surprised him given the fact that she'd caught him sleeping with her first love years before. *Maybe her mother mailed out the invites and sent me one by accident*, he thought. But he knew that wasn't true. The card was personally mailed to him with his name elegantly printed on top. Squeezing his eyes shut, Devin leaned against the seat with thoughts racing back to his teenage years and the friendship he'd had with Maya and Josh.

It was Maya who held his hand at his father's funeral. It was Josh who came over to play video games or basketball with him to keep his mind off the fact that his mother was a drunk. The two of them kept Devin company since his younger brother, Julian, was typically out smoking weed with friends or picking up girls— his preferred method of grieving, and his mother was either crying or passed out over her bed.

Devin was a popular kid, but even with all the girls pushing up on him, he preferred to hang around a small group of kids. He'd been friends with Maya and Josh, who'd been a couple, dating, since their freshman year.

In Josh, Devin found brotherhood, and with Maya he gained confidence. Following high school, the three of them ended up attending the same college. While Maya busied herself with pre-law coursework and sorority life, Devin and Josh got involved in school politics. Every so often Josh would complain about Maya never having time for him, but to fill that void he worked overtime to help Devin get elected to different campus leadership positions.

To get far away from the business that led to his father's

untimely death, Devin opted for politics and was named President of the Student Government Association during his junior year of college. He chose Josh as his chief of staff. Their time together steadily increased as they attended out of state recruitment trips and shared hotel rooms. During one trip, after an event in North Carolina, the two returned to their room and talked for hours. It was then that they shared their first kiss. At the time, Devin wasn't sure what that meant, and the pair quickly moved apart and carried on like nothing had happened. That was until the moment when their friendship went from brotherhood to romance in mere minutes. Details from that night still haunted Devin.

One evening, Maya, in an effort to spend more time with Josh, stopped by his apartment and found her longtime boyfriend and close friend, two men, having sex. This was the end of their friendship.

Besides a letter he sent to Maya, begging her not to share what happened with anyone, he'd had no further contact with her. With fears of being found out, Devin devoted the next few years to public service. He became an advocate for issues facing the black community and every mother's dream for their daughters. Having dated only women since that night, to that day he was still unsure of what his sexuality was.

Sitting back up, sweat continued to drip down his brow as his hands hugged the steering wheel so tightly that his knuckles turned a shade of red. Even though he'd arrived early, a quick glance at his clock indicated that the wedding ceremony was to begin in fifteen minutes. Devin knew he would either have to walk inside, or drive off. Though the latter seemed easier he knew he needed this closure.

Glancing into the rearview mirror, using the handkerchief from his front pocket, the attractive and stately man wiped the glistening splashes of anxiety from his forehead before exiting the car. It was now or never. With each step it felt like the world was closing in on him. His head began to spin and for a second, while heading up the stairway, he paused to steady his balance. Closing his eyes, he placed his hand on the stair rails and slowly raised one leather Armani shoe after the other. Pushing open the front door of the church, he headed to the chapel area, half-expecting guns to be blazing in his direction. Instead, he was met with cheerful chatter and loving eyes from friends and people he'd known for years. But he wasn't there to impress them, he was there for the bride.

Like a chameleon who could disguise itself at any turn, Devin hid his anxiety well and stopped to flash his mega-watt smile to the attendees, who recognized him immediately. He greeted a few familiar faces before settling onto a pew next to a former classmate, Tinsley Tyson. Tinsley had gone from being a reality star to a medical resident, and catching up with her was fascinating. It reminded Devin that it was never too late to start over.

The gentle murmurs came to an abrupt halt as the music cascaded throughout the room, signaling the start of the ceremony. The massive wooden doors to Calvary Baptist Church, the largest and most historical church in the city, opened, and the groom stood before the crowd of loved ones taking it all in. Smiling so hard that his gums were showing was a true indication that he was happy with his decision. After taking his spot next to the pastor, members of the bridal party began gliding down the aisle. Devin was delighted at the sight of Maya's long-lost brother, NBA player, Damien Roseland, who walked down the aisle and stood beside the groom. Maya and Damien had reconnected a few years earlier, after being separated for most of their lives, and it was nice to see that they'd remained close.

An hour later, Devin found himself in a tight embrace with Mr. and Mrs. Kincaid, family friends of nearly two decades. Though they seemed to be excited to see him, he noticed that two women dressed in matching bridesmaids' dresses standing close by, were not, and he knew why. Ivey and Taylor had been Maya's guard dogs for years, and his presence had them smelling blood. Deciding not to engage with them, in fear of starting a scene, Devin turned his back on them and continued talking to Maya's parents.

"How's your mother doing, dear?"

Slightly uncomfortable with the question, he knew Mrs. Kincaid knew good and well his mother wasn't okay and hadn't been the same since his father killed himself all those years ago. The two women had been in the same social circles for over a decade, and at one time were good friends.

"She's making it."

Before Devin was able to provide a fabricated update on his mother, the deejay blasted 24K Magic by Bruno Mars and out danced Maya and her husband, Corey. The night continued with no drama. Instead, Devin found himself really enjoying the energy and the company. A lot of people came over to congratulate him for the noise he was making on the political front. He was setting himself up to be in a position to run and win a national race, one day. After chopping it up with an old friend from college,

Devin looked around the room until he found who he was searching for.

Grabbing his sports coat from the back of his chair, he steadied his legs to walk in the direction of Maya, who sat alone at her table. There was no way Devin could leave without speaking to her. Halfway to her table, he was stopped by the two women he had noticed earlier, Taylor Desmond and Ivey Walden. Although Devin knew Ivey from back in the day when they attended the Bradwell Preparatory school with Maya, then later the same college, the two were never close.

"I still don't know why she invited your grimy ass," Taylor started, in her strong Philly accent.

"I'm more surprised he decided to show up. It's probably because he's running for something and needs to clean up his past," Ivey jumped in with her arms crossed. Always in the know, Ivey was a journalist and the star of a very successful talk show.

"My producer wanted me to reach out and ask you for an interview, as a young politician to watch out for, but I said hell no."

Both women were gorgeous, but in that moment their scowls had them looking like two extra's on the set of Jazmine Sullivan's music video for her hit song, *Bust Your Windows*. Devin was scared for his life.

"Y'all give the man some space," said a soft voice approaching the group.

Stepping between her best friends and their latest opponent, Maya gently took Devin by the hand and led him outside.

"You saved me," Devin mumbled.

Saying nothing, Maya simply offered up a smile. The wind picked up and her curls danced around her face. Always a gentleman, Devin took his jacket and placed it around her shoulders as they sat on a bench facing the lake.

"Congratulations, Maya, thank you so much for inviting me. My mom sends her love."

"Glad you could come. It's been a long time."

The one-time friends used to be able to talk all the time, but that was a long time ago, and now things were different.

"Maya, I never really apologized. What happened with Josh was a mistake. We hurt you. Then I had the nerve to turn around and ask you to keep everything a secret. I can't speak for him but I want you to know I'm truly sorry."

The sound of the wind filled the silence that followed. After a few seconds, Maya took Devin by the hand, once again, forcing him to look her in the eyes.

"You were scared," she began. "You were living a life in darkness. Not honest with yourself. It took me a while to really forgive you, but I did years ago, that's why I was able to invite you. Devin, make things right between us by being honest. You've been through a lot. You lost your dad when we were in high school. The buzz surrounding that still follows you wherever you go. And your mom…"

"Is a walking disaster," Devin interrupted with a chuckle to lighten the mood.

"Even with all that, look at you. You're in a position to do so much good! Politics is a tough game, give yourself some grace and let people know the real you. Everything done in the dark, comes to the light. All those years ago you asked me to not say anything about you being with Josh, and besides my girls, I never did. It wasn't about me protecting you, it was me giving you the opportunity to speak your own truth and on your own terms. Be honest with yourself before you even hit that national stage. Figure out who you are and what you want. If you lie, it will come out and destroy everything you've been working for. I've seen you with woman after woman. I don't know if you're being totally honest with them about who you are, but don't you dare do what you and Josh did to me, to someone else."

With that, Maya stood up and grabbed a shaken Devin into her arms. That was Maya, even on a day that was supposed to be all about her, all she wanted to do was to be there for someone else.

"You've got this," she whispered as she held her old friend in her arms for what seemed like forever.

Following his promise to Maya, a few months into his relationship with Vanessa, Devin admitted to her, his family and everyone who followed him online, that he was bisexual. A furious Vanessa parted ways with him immediately and spent days crying and wondering how she'd never seen the signs. But the truth was, there weren't any to see. Devin was the image of masculinity, and clearly defied all stereotypes of gay or bisexual men. Devin's previous relationship with Josh had been sparked by emotion that he just couldn't explain, and although he had found other men attractive since Josh, there never seemed to be enough of an emotional tie or connection for him to explore things further with them. Unsure of what this meant, Devin went to therapy to sort out his feelings. Months of self-work and honesty helped to catapult his confidence. He was finally comfortable in his own skin and ready to share his truth with the world.

Eventually, through some hard conversations, research and self-reflection, Vanessa decided that the love the two shared would be enough for them to get through anything, and she returned to the relationship. Her thoughts of—*What will people think about me? Will I be enough for him? Will I have to worry about him cheating on me with both women and men?*—were quieted as Devin worked overtime to reassure, love and show her that she was the woman he wanted by his side forever. She was confident that they could stand the test of time, which is why when he popped the question, she said yes.

His family didn't really seem to care. Mom was high when he first told her and all she asked was, "So you like 'em long and thick, hunh?"

Julian, his youngest brother, with his ignorant ass, asked, "Why? Were you touched when we were kids?"

Uncle Jacob just pounded Devin on the back, lit up a cigar and asked if he'd been watching the NBA finals. Having to respond to some of the questions he'd received had been annoying, but Devin managed to answer them all. To the public, he was just a fine, accomplished and rich black man. This became even more evident from all the support he was receiving since announcing his bid for a seat in the Senate. In all, Maya was right. Living in truth proved to be a good move.

The voice of his car companion brought Devin back to the present.

"Devin, Devin! Earth to Devin," Darlene called out to him. "We're here."

Darlene, who usually wore a stern expression, looked concerned, as if she were silently praying that Devin wasn't losing his mind this early in the race. Quickly gathering himself, within seconds, Devin presented his game face and was ready to go.

"I'm good, let's rock this next interview."

CHAPTER 5

DIGGING FOR GOLD

The attic was hard to navigate because of all the junk and dust crowding it, but somehow Ian found exactly what he was looking for in record time. The floor creaked below him as he grabbed a box from the top of a pile and slammed it to the ground. Dusting it off, the worn label with the name Thaddeus Simmons written on it, shone beneath the dirt. It had been years since he'd last opened it, and for a second, he paused.

What if I can't finish this? He thought to himself.

Arrogant by nature, compounded by his success, the veteran journalist quickly dismissed the idea and started figuring out how to get the heavy box downstairs. He was a lot younger when he first took it into the attic, and now he couldn't handle the weight. Luckily, his adult son Stephen was over for his weekly visit and could help.

An hour went by before Ian sat in his office sifting through news clippings and notes from the Paul Rucker and Thaddeus Simmons cases. Congressman Rucker was murdered in 2006, and famed businessman Thaddeus Simmons was accused of it. This was the one-story Ian could never finish. Seeing Thaddeus's son, Devin, on television had taken him back to the day Thaddeus was arrested for the murder of Congressman Paul Rucker, then later found dead in jail.

When the news broke of the late Congressman's murder, Ian had been in the middle of writing a story about a bribery ring that included many prominent businessmen and politicians, including Paul Rucker. He'd heard that Rucker was taking bribes in exchange for shaping legislation, and Ian had tried calling the Congressman for a quote, just to get the run around from his assistant. Two days after his last call, Ian found out the Congressman had been killed. The only witness to the crime was a prostitute who'd run away from the crime scene. Once he tracked her down, she claimed he had been murdered by a man who said he was sent by someone named Thaddeus Simmons.

According to the woman, whose name was Brittany Garcia, she had been picked up by Congressman Rucker in Logan Circle, an area in Washington, D.C. They drove to a dark alley where they snorted coke and made plans to have sex. As Rucker began to recline his seat, Brittany leaned over and lowered her head to his lap. Just as her mouth went to cover his member, a loud thumping noise came from the driver's side window, scaring her and causing her to bite down on his penis. Crying out in excruciating pain, Paul pushed her head away and unlocked his door to jump out and see where the disruption had come from.

Brittany said the bright lights from the open door illuminated a man dressed in all black standing at the car.

The next thing she remembered was the man pointing the gun at Paul before saying, "This is for Thaddeus." Her account was all the police needed to move in on Thaddeus Simmons. A raid of Simmons Enterprises unveiled a paper trail of illegal documents relating to Congressman Rucker, and although Brittany never identified Simmons as the killer, investigators were sure that it was a murder for hire scenario, so he was their main suspect. Before he could make it to trial, Thaddeus was found hanging in his cell, and his death was ruled a suicide.

Years later, Ian still could not wrap his mind around Thaddeus's involvement in Paul Rucker's death. It just didn't add up, especially since he later learned that Thaddeus was working with the feds on another case. He couldn't understand why Thaddeus would risk his own deal with the FBI to have Rucker killed, or why the girl who was with Rucker was kept alive. Thaddeus was a sharp businessman and a former officer in the military who had served his country in war. He was known to be a ladies' man who notoriously cheated on his wife and occasionally took part in backroom business deals, but Ian had never gotten the sense that he was capable of orchestrating an assassination.

"I think whoever had Rucker killed, then killed Thaddeus in prison and staged it as suicide," Ian mumbled to himself.

Hanging up the small collage of key players that he'd started over fifteen years ago, Ian took a step back and examined the photos on the board. His eyebrows furrowed as he slowly went over one face after the other. When Ian prepared for a story, he went after it with everything he had and was as meticulous with his findings as a doctor diagnosing a patient. From Thaddeus, he glanced to the people surrounding his name—Jacob, Paul, Brenda, FBI Special Agent Charles Welsh and Brittany. Letting out a loud snarl, Ian turned around and threw his hands over his face in frustration. He was still missing something, or more importantly, someone.

"Hey, Dad, here's the latest copy of *Impact* magazine. It's the most influential people issue," interrupted Stephen, who stood in the doorway. Eleven years had passed since Ian's ex-wife divorced him, citing irreconcilable differences. To her, Ian worked too much and gave their marriage too little, and he agreed. Although Stephen knew his dad appreciated the space the divorce allotted him, he still made it a point to check on his father every week, and was pleased to see he was knee-deep in a new assignment. Staring at the medley of photos his dad had up in the office, Stephen, knew he would have to increase his visits to twice a week.

"Thaddeus Simmons? You're back on him?"

Ignoring his son's inquiry, Ian took the magazine and closed the door on his son, who waited for answers. Sitting down at his desk, Ian figured a break was needed. Flipping the magazine open to no page in particular, the face that stared back at him made him jump in his seat. Puzzle pieces flew around in his head as his mind began sorting out the unknown. On the glossy page before him, a man long believed to be involved in some of the biggest scandals in politics and business, who was ironically pretty close with Thaddeus, and had been chummy with Congressman Rucker, stared back at him. How had he missed this?

"Regis fucking Adams."

CHAPTER 6

HOSTESS DOIN' THE MOSTEST

A couple of months had flown by since Devin announced his candidacy, and even with the rigorous schedule that now took over his life, he was overjoyed by his reception. The celebration continued with famed artists and community activists such as rapper Meek Mill and Cory Booker rallying behind the young candidate, throwing parties and dinners on his behalf. Unfortunately, there was still one more party happening that Devin wasn't too excited about. His mother's. After dodging her calls and texts Devin finally responded to his mother's request to host a dinner party in his honor.

Now, sitting in the car heading south towards Loudon County, an affluent part of Virginia that was little more than an hour away, he regretted giving in to her. Approaching the gate that led to the estate, Devin braced himself for what was to come. While the valet attendant opened Vanessa's door, Devin contemplated turning around and heading home. Against his better judgment he got out of the car, grabbed his suit jacket from the backseat and handed the keys to the attendant. Taking Vanessa's hand, he led her to the front entrance where music could be heard from outside. Planting a fake smile on his lips, he walked confidently up the front steps of the residence. It still amazed him that the government hadn't been able to seize the house in Virginia following his father's incarceration.

As soon as he walked through the door his worst nightmare came true. Standing in the foyer, looking high as a kite, was his mother. Barely able to keep herself from falling over, she leaned against the banister of the spiral staircase, attempting to greet guests in what she must have hoped was a dignified manner. Glancing up from her conversation with someone Devin had never met, she shrieked and ran to hug her son and future daughter-in-law. The fake smile remained steady as Devin hugged his mother, while trying to stop her from falling over at the same time.

"Honey, isn't this beautiful? And it's all for you," she slurred.

Before he could respond, Vanessa jumped in the conversation.

"You're looking beautiful tonight Mrs. Simmons."

"It's Miss, dear. That weak sonofabitch killed himself years ago, so I'm a single woman now."

As her voice rose an octave, nearby guests turned towards the trio and their conversation. Noticing the attention, Brenda winked at a man in the crowd who was staring and shaking his head. At the right moment, Julian Simmons appeared at the top of the stairs with a woman, as usual, on his arm. Hearing his mother spouting off, he released his date's arm and went to help his big brother tame her.

Brenda Simmons was a poor sight. The death of her husband had hit her the hardest, both emotionally and mentally. By sheer luck, even though the government did take a sizable amount of their assets, after confirming foul play in a few past business deals organized by Thaddeus, it hadn't seized all of their money and possessions, so Brenda and the boys had been able to maintain a certain financial lifestyle. These comforts didn't stop her from self-destructing. Her best friend was Xanax and her medicine included vodka martinis. It was no secret that even before Thad died she was a heavy drinker, some would say borderline alcoholic. When they were kids, Brenda used to tell the boys, "I drink because your daddy can't keep his zipper up."

The boys didn't know what that meant until a boy from school filled them in on all the cheating their father had done over the years, sometimes even with their teachers. It finally started to make sense to them. All the arguments their parents had had over their father coming home late, or his insistence that he go on business trips alone—were because of other women. In time, the boys realized the issue was deeper than that. Brenda had a problem, and Thaddeus was tired of it.

Naturally a small woman, their mother dropped an additional thirty pounds following her husband's death, leaving her at a whopping 104 pounds. She appeared to be sick. Looking her over, Devin was disgusted by what he saw. He still remembered the days of his buddies talking about how beautiful she was, and in return threatening them to stay away from his mama. Brenda Simmons had been something special. Physically, she had been built like what Uncle Jacob used to call a brick house, and to top it off she had graduated top of her class from two prominent institutions, so she was no dummy.

Born in the Bronx, Brenda came from a middle-class family, with an emphasis on family. She, along with her parents and two sisters, shared a duplex with a total of nine people. There was never a quiet moment in the home. The adults would work throughout the week and the kids went to school, but after seven at night, it was party time in the Davis household. Brenda would watch her aunts and uncles play spades, shoot dice on the porch and blast music that could be heard all the way down the street. Liquor was always flowing and food was plentiful. Even though the party nights would start with innocent fun, they usually ended in fights, threats, and occasionally, a police officer or two. For a long time, Brenda, would go outside and hang out with her cousins and kids from the neighborhood, but that all stopped when she reached tenth grade. She began filling out in what some would say, all the right places, but as beautiful and shapely as she was, she had both street and classroom smarts. She focused on using school as a way for her to get the life she had always dreamed of. She loved her family, and while they weren't poor, she wanted more for herself. That ambition landed her a full scholarship to New York University, then Columbia, where she studied international law.

On her way home from class one day during her final

year of law school, Brenda met a man who would later change the whole trajectory of her life.

The two first met while waiting for a cab in New York. Thaddeus, originally from Georgia, with all the qualities of a southern gentleman, offered her a taxi that had stopped in front of them. The small gesture was attractive to Brenda. Rarely did anyone give up their taxi once they were able to hail one. Wanting to find out who this mystery man was, she suggested they share it. It was then that Thaddeus, whom she later learned was an officer in the military, currently stationed at the Pentagon, worked his charm and won her over. The two eventually married, and Brenda, who decided to put her law career on hold, left New York to join Thaddeus in Washington, D.C.

Things were good for the first decade, then it all went to hell. Thaddeus left the military and the District of Columbia, and started his own arms, defense, information security and technology company in Maryland. Devin and Julian were born and, at first, the couple was more in love than ever. But as the company grew, Brenda and Thaddeus became more and more distant. Date nights were spent at networking and work events. Conversations were limited as Thaddeus spent most of his time on the phone working out deals that would prove fruitful, or was in the office until the wee hours of the morning, leaving Brenda at home alone with two young boys. To cope with the changes, Brenda started drinking heavily, and Thaddeus's work trips began to increase.

At nine-years-old, Devin became the man of the house since his dad was always away on business and his mom was always inebriated. Devin could never get one distinct image of his mother out of his head. He recalled the night he found her naked in their Olympic size pool. On that night, once he had made sure Julian was sound asleep, he'd headed to his mother's room to say goodnight. Normally, she was in bed watching her TV shows and was barely lucid. After peeking his head inside her dimly lit room, he realized the music in the backyard must be where she had gone for the night.

Wiping his eyes sleepily, Devin groaned and stomped down the stairs to see what his mom was up to. Rounding the corner, he stopped to stare at the sight in front of him. Not only was his mom naked, but she was floating face down in the pool, motionless. With his father out of town, Devin raced to pull his mother out, then called Uncle Jacob for help with her when he noticed she was still breathing. They had acquired a great deal of wealth by this time and calling the paramedics or the police was a no-no. Mom's shenanigans had to be kept in-house.

Uncle Jacob came over that night with an on-call doctor, and stayed by Brenda's side until the morning. He'd always had a soft spot for his late best friend's wife, and would stop everything whenever she called or needed him. In spite of her drinking, he still found her to be an amazing woman who just needed some love and help.

The next day, Brenda, weak and tired, was sent to rehab. She went four more times over the years, but all to no avail. The boys constantly found bottles stashed around the house, were always on edge pending their mother's mood and were scared every time they found her passed out. She needed help but no one knew what to do.

Today, things were even worse.

"Mama, come with me," Julian said. The younger son was somewhat of a mama's boy. Even with all that their mother had put them through, he always had faith that one day she would get better. Taking her by the arm, he steered Brenda out of the room as he and Devin had had to do a million times before at gatherings. As the two walked away, Vanessa grabbed Devin by the hand and squeezed it. Devin wanted to leave the party right then and there, but knew it wouldn't be a good look. Instead, he went about the rest of the night as if everything were normal. Julian came back to the group half an hour later. Having found his date, he then walked towards Devin and quietly whispered, "She's asleep."

For half an hour, Julian sat with their mother, stroking her hair in the downstairs guestroom until she fell asleep on top of the neatly made bed. Even though he should have been used to doing this, every time it happened he was brought back down to his knees, emotionally exhausted.

"Something needs to change bro," Devin whispered back.

"Man, she has to want it. After all this time I still don't think she does."

Devin knew he was right, but in that moment all he felt was anger. The night went on, and the spirited conversation, good food and drinks blurred out the fact that the hostess was long gone and passed out in a nearby room.

CHAPTER 7

HELP HAS ARRIVED

The next day, a game show blasted from a television in the bedroom next door, waking Devin. For a second, he couldn't remember where he was. Taking in the painting that hung on the wall closest to his nightstand, he let out a breath.

"Mom's house," he mumbled to himself.

The events from the night before flooded back into memory. After a long evening, Vanessa and Devin decided to stay at the estate instead of heading back home. Usually, Devin wanted to get far away from his mother at the first opportunity, but Vanessa, who made sure to pack overnight bags just in case, insisted they stay to check on her the next morning. Always the thoughtful one, something he admired about her, Devin gave in. The empty space with wrinkled sheets next to him let him know that his lover was already up and moving around. Throwing on a t-shirt and basketball shorts, Devin brushed his teeth and prepared for the storm that was Hurricane Brenda.

Devin came out of his room at the same time as Julian.

"You stayed too?" Devin asked while dapping up his brother.

"Yeah, I put my date in a car, and figured I'd stay behind to be with Mom for a couple of days."

"I don't know how you do it, man. You always put up with her shit."

"What am I supposed to do? You're busy with the campaign, and I have some free time. I'm not about to sit around and let her kill herself."

"You may not have noticed, but she's killing herself even with you here."

Ignoring his big brother, Julian started heading down the stairs. From the downstairs guestroom came laughter. Peeking inside, the brothers saw Vanessa and their mother engaged in a deep conversation. Brenda still looked sick, but for the moment she was somewhat sober.

Noticing the two brothers looking in, Vanessa called for them to enter.

"Your mom was just telling me how she hasn't been to Houston in years. She wants to go back for a visit."

Devin could care less where she wanted to visit, getting the fuck up out of that house and away from that woman was the only thing on his mind. Instead of voicing his true feelings, he twisted his face in disgust.

"What do you want to do in Texas, Mom?" Julian asked.

Brenda looked down and hesitated, allowing Vanessa to continue.

"My cousin has some land outside of Houston. It's peaceful and a great place to be when you need an escape. I think it would be a perfect place for Brenda to go to get away from the city."

Devin was already through with the conversation. His mother didn't need a trip, she needed Jesus. Turning to walk back upstairs, he stopped when his mother quickly looked up and apologized, "I'm really sorry, Devin. Yesterday was supposed to be for you and I ruined it. I didn't mean to, I don't know what happened."

It was at that moment that Devin went from 0 to 100.

"Mom, not only did you throw a party that no one asked you to throw, but you acted a damn fool! You never fucking know what happened. Aren't you tired of being talked about? Don't you have any shame? Have you stopped to look in the mirror? You're like a skeleton walking! One drink or pill away from death!"

With that, he about-faced and marched back to his room, taking two stairs at a time, with Vanessa scurrying behind him. Throwing his bag on the bed, he remained silent as Vanessa continued the conversation that had started downstairs.

"Babe, I really think you should listen. Houston could be good for your mom."

Devin paused from folding his briefs, looked Vanessa square in the face with eyes blazing and spoke bluntly.

"Vanessa, are you coming with me or would you rather stay with Julian to babysit that grown ass woman downstairs? I'm out of here either way."

For a second Vanessa remained still. She could tell Devin was mad, he rarely got like that. Even though she wanted to stay and help her soon to be mother-in-law, she knew it was best to ride home with Devin, especially considering the state he was in. She decided to work on Brenda's behalf from home. Reaching for her Ebby Rane luggage, she quietly began to pack. Ten minutes later, without so much as a goodbye, the couple was out the door and on the expressway, headed home.

Days went by, and Devin carried on as if nothing had happened. He whistled in the mornings, laughed at nothing and danced around the house as if to prove he was okay. Late one evening, Vanessa was lying in bed reading a book when Devin walked in, blasting Whitney Houston, *I Wanna Dance with Somebody*. Grabbing her from the bed, he twirled her around until both of them were dizzy and falling over with laughter. Vanessa loved his bubbly mood but was worried about his emotional state. For years, his mother had weighed heavily on his mind. Vanessa was sure he was just masking his emotions, but didn't dare bring up her concerns.

On the fourth day, she discreetly made calls to her cousin in Houston, as well as to Julian, to arrange for Brenda to fly out of Dulles Airport to Houston Hobby. Not only would she be far away from an upset Devin, but she could get some real help. Help that rehab hadn't been able to accomplish. Vanessa hadn't mentioned it to Brenda, but her cousin was an addict who'd been recovered for almost two decades. She was certain that being out in the country with him would yield good results.

CHAPTER 8

CERTIFIED LOVER BOY

Unlike Devin, who had a knack for politics and an interest in public service, Julian Simmons was all about his money and himself. Following in his father's footsteps, Julian joined Grayson Holdings, formerly Simmons Enterprises, as a result of the scandal, and became Jacob's shadow. After attending The Wharton School of the University of Pennsylvania he went to work for the company as Chief Financial Officer. He was young, rich and a bachelor in its purest form. He was living a life most men his age prayed for, and he knew it. Leaning back in his chair and placing his feet on the desk, Julian reached for his phone to send a text confirming his mom's travel arrangements with Vanessa.

Once sent, he decided to make a quick call to Jade to cancel his plans with her for the night. As luck had it, his old girlfriend from college was in town and wanted to see him. He would never admit this to anyone, but Avery Jones was the one who got away. Four years after their breakup she still did something to him that no other woman had been able to do, and that was to love. Her last-minute business trip was bringing her from Los Angeles to D.C. for one week only and he wasn't going to miss the chance to see her.

"Hello," purred the voice on the other end of the line.

"Hey baby, I'm sorry but I have to work late. Not going to make it over."

Instantly, Jade went from soft to stern.

"Julian, you promised you'd come over after you cancelled Tuesday."

"I know, but Uncle Jacob got me working on a last-minute project," Julian swiftly lied.

"Ugh, shouldn't you be the boss of the company? I mean your daddy founded it."

Rolling his eyes, Julian tried to remind himself why he was entertaining Jade to begin with, then quickly remembered. She was a nag and a gold digger, but she was thick as hell and her head game was tough.

"I'm going to make it up to you, baby, believe that."

After a few more seconds of reassuring her he'd be over the next day, Julian hung up and called out to his assistant. An older woman entered the room with a notepad that was always glued to her hands. When it came to Julian, his requests were always outlandish, and it was better to write it all down than to try and remember.

"Please send Jade some chocolates from that dessert place she likes in Bethesda."

Donna had been Julian's assistant for the last few years and was well aware of his bachelor lifestyle. It seemed like every other day she was scheduling a dinner or an activity for a new girl. At first, working for a playboy made her uncomfortable, but after she deposited her first check, with the extra zero on it, she concluded that at fifty-six she didn't care, as long as her check cleared and she was home by 6 p.m. every day.

"I'll get that done. Also, Mr. Grayson called and needs you in his office before you leave for the day."

Hoping this wouldn't take all night, Julian stood up and reached for his briefcase and coat.

"Thank you, Donna, get home safe. I'll see you in the morning."

With that, the young executive walked up the hall to his uncle's office. Rounding the corner, Julian noticed the door to his uncle's office was cracked open. He could see his uncle speaking into the receiver of his phone. The anger on his face made Julian stop, mid-step. When Jacob was mad, all hell broke loose. People either got fired or cussed out. Julian had learned his lesson after the first time he decided to test his uncle.

Just four months after joining the company, Julian was notorious for consistently showing up to work late and leaving early, falling asleep during important meetings and ogling every woman's ass that he passed in the halls, even Katie's and she didn't have an ass to look at. On the night of the company holiday party, Julian returned to the office, which was just five blocks from the party venue, with Alana, the event planner by his side. At the party, it had not taken Julian long to zero in on the Indian cutie, and when she accidentally bumped into him, he knew it was going to be a good night.

Opting for his uncle's office, since it had the most space and he had a key, Julian laid Alana on top of the desk, pushing plaques, pictures and papers to the side to make room for the two of them. Not even twenty minutes in, with his face cloaked between her legs, Julian felt his entire body tighten while a piercing vibration shook his brain like it was a peanut in a jar. Unable to think or see clearly, he was convinced that he was dying.

Falling onto the floor, he lay there with a ringing in his ear and blurry images clouding his vision. What seemed like hours went by before he was able to make out the figure standing over him. It was Uncle Jacob, pointing at him, bellowing, with a stun gun in his hand. Finally, reality set in as he noticed his pants laid out on the ground to his left and the faint smell of Alana's perfume.

"Boy, are you stupid? This is a billion-dollar business. You didn't think I had cameras in this mutherfucker? Get y'all nasty asses up and clean up my shit!"

Julian had never seen his uncle that upset, and had never been the recipient of his fury. Realizing that Alana had bolted from the room, he immediately wished he had escaped with her. After cleaning up the office, with the constant ringing still in his ear, he saw Jacob came back into the office, holding a pair of women's size four panties.

"I found them in the hallway, figured you'd want to keep them to remember the day you learned not to fuckin disrespect me."

Tossing the underwear to Julian, Jacob turned around and walked to the garage, letting Julian's *sorry* fall on deaf ears

Deciding to dodge his uncle for the day, Julian, started to turn around and leave, until he heard Jacob say something interesting.

"I don't know what you want from me. I told you before, I have nothing to tell the reporter. Thaddeus didn't tell me anything about you or that side of the business, so I'm not understanding what I have to do with any of this."

Jacob's voice trailed off and he listened, as if receiving information from whomever was on the phone. Finally, slamming the iPhone down on his desk, he covered his face with his hands in defeat. Julian took that moment to silently head towards the elevator. Jacob mentioning his father stayed on Julian's mind as he entered the elevator, until his phone buzzed with a text from Avery.

Avery: Can't wait to see you.

Replying with a heart, Julian forgot all about what his uncle was saying and, instead, focused on his date for the night with Avery Jones.

CHAPTER 9

PAST MEETS PRESENT

"I don't even know why I'm here," Jacob murmured into his glass of scotch as he sat alone at the bar.

Two hours had passed since he'd received the news that the well-known journalist Ian Thompson was poking around and asking questions about his late best friend, Thaddeus. For the last thirty-five minutes he'd been sitting inside a low-key pub in Prince George's County waiting to meet an acquaintance, and Jacob was beginning to grow impatient with each minute that passed.

Almost as soon as he glanced down at his wristwatch for the fourth time, the door to the small establishment opened and an older gentleman with a thin frame walked through it.

At first glance, Regis Adams appeared to be small in stature, but many quickly learned what he lacked in size, he more than made up for in power. As one of D.C.'s most powerful but discreet figures, Regis was known for his political influence and business acumen. Throughout his decades-long career, Regis had acted as a political consultant, policy advisor to the president, lobbyist—and then board member to several fortune 500 companies. He was well connected, respected, rich, and to Jacob, dangerous. Few spoke of the rumors, but Regis's name had been used in connection with blackmail, corruption and murder. He was a formidable figure.

"Jacob, it's nice to see you again," said Regis, approaching the bar.

Standing to greet him, Jacob shook the man's frail but strong grip before grabbing his wallet off the bar and motioning to the server to guide them to their table.

Once the server retreated to get their drinks, Jacob launched into an apology.

"Regis, I apologize for my tone earlier, the news caught me by surprise. Just like I told you years ago, I don't know anything, so I have nothing to share with anyone if they ask."

For a second, Regis gathered his hands in front of him on the small table and studied the younger man sitting across from him. Within seconds, he had taken in Jacob's nervousness, his mood and every item of clothing he had on him. His photographic memory and ability to read people made him a quick but efficient observer. Folding his hands into his lap, he was pleased to see the fear in Jacob's eyes.

"It's alright Jacob, but I'm afraid we have a real problem here. You see, I think you know more than you let on, and that's an issue for me. That journalist is digging around, asking questions, which means soon the feds will be digging too and I need to make sure I'm dotting all my I's and crossing all my T's. Somehow, my name has gotten mixed in with Thaddeus's and Paul's and that's not good for my business."

Sitting back to let his words sink in, Regis knew he had Jacob rattled.

Jacob had always known Regis was somehow involved in the scandal that eventually led his late friend to an early grave, but just knowing what Regis was capable of and the danger he was to Thaddeus's family and his own, Jacob made the decision to keep his opinions to himself years ago. Shrinking under his stare, Jacob had been ready to pack a bag that night and leave the country, but thought better of it. He knew he wouldn't be able to even make it to Canada without Regis being alerted.

To gently remind Jacob what was at stake, Regis leaned forward, forcing Jacob's diverted eyes to meet his.

"I don't know what all Thaddeus shared with you before he killed himself, but it's in your best interest to keep it to yourself." For a second, Regis picked up his glass of water and smirked. "Did I mention all the money I've been able to get for Devin's campaign?"

At the mention of his godson, Jacob sat up straighter. "Like I told you before, you don't have to worry about me, Regis."

Across town at a pool hall, Ian Thompson, had a meeting of his own. The thought of Regis Adams being somehow involved drummed up an old ally in FBI Special Agent, Charles Welsh, who had been present at the raid of Thaddeus's office all those years ago. He was also one of the few people who questioned the charges against the fallen businessman. While the world was ready to tarnish the name of Thaddeus Simmons, Welsh had refused to do so, and one might say he was crippled and demoted to desk duty at the bureau because of it. Since then, Ian had remained in contact with Welsh, and occasionally asked for his insight on cases for articles he was writing. The shunned federal agent leaned forward in his wheelchair with his eyes on the corner pocket, and made his shot.

"Give me my money, Ian, and tell me why you got me at this dump."

Welsh placed his cue stick down and waited for an explanation. Instead of launching into his theories and questioning, Ian had thought it better to play a round of pool and drink some beers to lighten the mood, but it was finally time for him to open up to Welsh. Taking a swig of his drink, Ian casually mentioned seeing Thaddeus's oldest son on television.

"I heard Devin Simmons's announcement the other day. He's trying to take one of the open Senate seats in Maryland."

"Okay, so?"

"So, it got me thinking. Tell me, have you stopped thinking about what really happened to Thaddeus?"

Looking away from Ian's probing stare, Welsh grabbed his hat off the nearby table and prepared to leave.

"That case has been closed, Ian, give it a rest."

"But no, it hasn't, and before you run out of here like a little wimp, tell me, how much do you know about Regis Adams?"

Teeth gritted, Welsh yanked the collar of the nosy journalist and pulled him down toward his seated position until they were close enough to feel each other's breath.

"Are you trying to get us killed?" he barked quietly.

Welsh knew first-hand what looking into the likes of Regis Adams could do. Once a star at the bureau, Welsh was now relegated to a wheelchair and typed reports for a living. He missed his days in the field where he had worked on some of the biggest cases of the century, ranging from public corruption and white-collar crimes to violent crimes and foreign counterintelligence. Those days came to an abrupt halt the day he was run off the road on his way back to D.C. from the backwoods of Virginia. He'd been out there to hunt down the witness from the Paul Rucker case. He'd received a tip that Brittany Garcia was hiding from the press in that area. The bureau hadn't sanctioned his search so he was on his own with no backup.

A little past ten p.m. on a cold November day, he was going down a dark winding road, when bright headlights appeared behind him from a car going at a highspeed. In an effort to avoid a collision, Welsh, who sped up and made a sharp right turn, headed straight for a tree, knocking himself out cold. When he woke up he was in a hospital bed with his wife crying quietly by his side. Oblivious to what had happened, he tried jumping out of the bed before he realized there was no feeling in his legs. He was paralyzed from the waist down.

In the months that followed his recovery, he received a visit from a top official at the bureau and quickly learned that the house call wasn't to check on his recovery but to assess what information he had on his cases. Too smart to fall for the inquiry, he kept his answers on the status of his ongoing cases short, but before the high-level official left, he bluntly told Welsh to leave the Thaddeus Simmons and Paul Rucker cases alone. It was then that he realized his near-death experience wasn't an accident.

"Don't call me about this shit anymore."

With that, Welsh wheeled off towards the door, leaving Ian behind, hopefully for good.

CHAPTER 10

DOUBLE DATE

Cherry blossoms were popping up all around the city, signaling that spring was here. For Devin, this meant that election day was only eight months away and there was still a lot of work to do if he wanted to capture the votes needed to win a Senate seat. For Vanessa, it meant the wedding would be here in only six months. The couple would have been happy to host a small wedding after the election, but Darlene thought having it before would make for great optics, adding more work and stress for them all.

Between campaign commitments, wedding planning, plus Vanessa's philanthropic work, quality time together was hard to come by. This was why, when Devin got a text from Julian asking if he and Vanessa were free that night for a double date at a new upscale lounge that had recently opened near the Inner Harbor, he jumped at the idea. It was the only night they had available for the week. Even though they were both tired, they knew a night out was needed to keep the spark in their relationship.

Pulling up outside the venue, Devin knew that even though it was supposed to be a relaxing evening, he was still very much on the campaign trail. In true Darlene fashion, a photographer was posted outside the lounge, ready to photograph Vanessa and him for the media. A beautiful black power couple out on the town would make them endearing to voters, so said the strategic campaign manager. Valet took their car at the same time Julian rolled up in his loud bright orange, Lamborghini.

"Can he go anywhere and not be flashy?" laughed Vanessa. The two stood to the side and waited for Julian and his date to get out.

"He can't help himself. I swear he thinks he's Hugh Hefner. I wonder who he brought with him this time."

On cue, Avery Jones stepped out of the passenger side of the exotic automobile with the help of an attendant. Pleasantly surprised, Vanessa rushed towards his date and threw her arms around Avery for a tight hug. Avery was a family favorite, whom they rarely saw since she lived in California.

"What are you doing in town?" began Vanessa.

"Work, but I'll tell you more inside," grinned Avery. She'd always loved Julian's family and enjoyed being around Vanessa, even though it wasn't often. Greetings were given, and the three, led by Julian, who walked like he owned the place, started towards the entrance.

A camera went off as Devin's younger brother flashed a bright smile in the direction of the cameraman. The good thing about being the brother of a politician, and not a politician, was the free publicity, and Julian used this to promote products and brands on his social media. Flicking her finger on the backside of his head like she had been doing to him since their college days, Avery motioned for her self-absorbed ex to walk more and pose less. Massaging the sore spot he now had on the back of his head, Julian shot her a dirty look and headed inside.

"I need to try that on Devin when he's watching football and ignoring me," laughed Vanessa.

"I probably wouldn't even feel it, if it's the Ravens playing," teased Devin in a raised voice so he could be heard over the band. Within minutes, the group was settled in a booth. Drink orders were given and they leaned back to enjoy the group performing on stage. While the women caught up with each other, Devin leaned across the table to his brother.

"So, what's been up?" Devin asked, with a side glance towards Avery.

Julian knew he was referring to the beautiful chocolate woman sitting next to him, but that was a conversation for another day.

"Man, we'll talk about that later," he grinned.

Devin wished that instead of whoring around town with gold diggers like the girl Jade, that Julian would commit to someone special like Avery.

"I see you're still a man-child," said Devin as he shook his head. "What about work? I feel like I'm always talking about this campaign, so I want to talk about something else for a change. It's nice to hang out and not be on for the cameras."

Julian could understand that, and even though he liked attention and had been approached for acting gigs a few times, he never wanted the amount of attention that running for public office or being on television would give him.

"Well, I don't know how much Vanessa's been telling you about Mom, but she's doing well down in Houston."

Devin raised a hand to stop the conversation before it continued. Julian knew not to keep going and closed his mouth. After a brief pause, a thought came to him and he recalled leaving the office a week before and hearing Uncle Jacob mention their father's name.

"Here's something for you, a few days ago I heard Uncle Jacob on the phone, and he sounded paranoid and upset."

Leaning forward to hear more, Devin waited for his brother to continue.

"Bro it was weird. Whoever he was talking to, they were discussing Dad, and I could have heard his tone wrong, but it sounded like the person on the other end of the call was threatening him."

"Well, what about Dad?" Devin asked.

"That's the thing, I couldn't catch everything and I was on my way out to meet Avery, but what I did hear was something about someone looking into Dad's old case."

Before Devin could respond, Vanessa interrupted.

"Oh babe, tell Avery that our photos are going to be in *Essence*, she doesn't believe me."

For the time being, Devin tabled his reply and focused on his wife-to-be, who was squealing with excitement over their wedding spread being in the iconic magazine.

"It's true," he laughed.

CHAPTER 11

MS. AVERY JONES

Shielding his eyes from the light that was shining inside the house, Julian sat up and placed his arms above him to release a long yawn. Next to him, Avery Jones, his first love, stirred briefly in her sleep. Kissing her forehead, Julian stood up from the bed and quickly made the decision to surprise Avery with breakfast. Unlike Devin, who depended on Vanessa and Ms. Ruby for all his meals, Julian took pride in cooking. A lot of people were surprised to learn that this bachelor, in all his bachelor-pad glory, had a set of cookware that could rival Michelin Star chef, Mariya Russell's.

Just as he was finishing up the French toast, Avery appeared, looking fresh and happy, wearing one of Julian's, Penn t-shirts. Coming around the island, she leaned over his shoulder to take a peek at what he was cooking. Pleased to see that it was one of her favorite breakfast dishes, she quickly grabbed a piece of bacon from a plate and ran, before Julian could take it from her. With a spatula in his hand, he waved for Avery to put the pork back down.

Ignoring his command, she took a seat at the kitchen table and watched Julian as he finished up breakfast. She couldn't believe how in-sync they always were, even after all these years of living cross country. Though they made sure to always keep in touch, they weren't totally current on everything going on in each other's lives.

"Last night was fun, it was nice to see Devin and Vanessa. But talk to me, tell me how you've been," said Avery, as Julian started to place items on the table.

"What do you want me to say? All I do is work."

"Well, that's a lie," said Avery as she thought about the picture she saw of him recently on social media. The picture was taken at a club just two weeks prior, and showed a smiling Julian flanked on either side by a couple of girls dressed like strippers. Reading her mind, Julian, quickly explained that he only went out when international clients and partners came to town. Rolling her eyes, Avery just responded with a smirk.

"Seriously, Avery, I've slowed down a lot."

"Really? So, you're not seeing anyone right now?"

"Why do you care, aren't you still dating that techie out in California?"

"If I was, do you think I would've slept with you last night? You know I've never been that girl. I can only deal with one man at a time."

"True," said Julian with a pause.

At that moment, a banging noise came from outside his condominium. Running to the door at the sound of someone screaming, Avery stood up from the table to follow Julian. Peeking through the peephole, his mouth dropped open and he couldn't move. Avery pushed him to the side to see what was going on. For a moment she saw a woman on the other side of the door, then she heard a spraying noise and a substance quickly clouded her view.

"Bring your ass out here, Julian, you and that bitch!"

Jade, in all her big booty glory was there, and it was clear that she had no plans of leaving any time soon.

"You got to be fucking kidding me," Avery said. "You're still on this shit? Fucking crazy hoes, then acting surprised when they get crazy on you?"

Totally forgetting that Jade was on the building's guest list, it made sense that she was able to get past security without a call to Julian to verify her. Walking back to the kitchen to grab his phone, he called security to handle the situation. Ten minutes later, two beefy guards showed up to escort a kicking and screaming Jade out of the high-priced building. After a few seconds Julian and Avery retreated back to the kitchen and sat down.

"Every time I see you it starts off great. We have a good time and even better conversation. I always start thinking about how things would be if we were to get back together, and then shit like this happens and I'm reminded that crazy bitches follow you everywhere you go."

Julian knew she was referring to the time she had to fight a girl when they were in grad school because he had been cheating.

"Avery, I—"

"Don't, Julian, let me get dressed, then take me to the airport."

Avery stood up from the table and left the room. She'd lost her appetite.

CHAPTER 12

MO' MONEY, MO' PROBLEMS

The office space bustled with activity as staff and volunteers of all ages came together for the sole mission of getting Devin Simmons elected to Congress. In his office, Devin was busy with meetings and calls for the entire morning before making a scheduled appearance at Morgan State University.

"Regis, I can't thank you enough for all the support you've given me over the past year. Your personal donation was astounding, and now my finance director says you have a new list of potential donors. I can never repay you for this."

"Just win," laughed Regis Adams, on the other end of the line.

Because of the political powerhouse, Devin was able to raise more than $15 million towards his campaign in just a few months, and that figure grew daily. As kids, Devin and his brother, Julian, had considered Regis to be a mean old man, but as the years following the death and scandal of their father passed, so had their opinion of him. The boys matured well, and Regis remained present in their lives, seeing to it that they were well taken care of. He knew their mother was in no shape to properly care for his late friend's sons, so even though Jacob stayed close and acted as a second father, it was Regis who made sure they attended the best schools and knew all the right people, doing so from a distance. As kids, they had annoyed him, but now that they were adults, he had developed a fondness for them, despite the hairy relationship he'd had with their father in his last days.

Devin appreciated the interest Regis was taking in his campaign, and was very aware that he had a heavy hitter supporting him. It was widely known that Regis was well respected in politics and business. Aware of the whispers surrounding him, and some of the unsavory things people said he may have done, Devin had never seen Regis act in any way other than as the powerful man he was.

"I promise to do my best," said Devin, wanting to make him proud, and he meant it.

The campus of Morgan State University was busy, as students rushed to make evening classes, meet with friends or attend study group sessions. Darlene had set up a campus visit and rally to introduce Devin to the students at the college. He'd already visited the University of Maryland and Coppin State the week before, so he was familiar with how the rally would run and the types of questions to expect. He was excited to see the students who were all potential voters.

Walking into the auditorium, the crowd erupted in cheers. Overwhelmed by the reception he received, Devin took a moment to take in all the black excellence that surrounded him. He felt right at home and was grateful for the amount of love he was receiving. To top things off, he was being introduced by April Ryan, graduate of Morgan State, and former White House correspondent and CNN political analyst. For the first ten minutes, the band played and students rocked the stands, dancing and having a good time. They'd heard Devin on the Breakfast Club, had seen celebrities promoting him, and knew his race would be a historic victory if he won and became the first African American, United States Senator from Maryland. Excited to have him on their campus, the students made sure to make him feel their support. Sororities and fraternities showed up in droves, remaining towards the front of the stage and representing in their colors. The atmosphere was live, and for a second Devin wondered if he was in a scene from the TV show, *A Different World*.

Finally, the band concluded their set and April Ryan came to the stage to introduce Devin. As April talked and reminisced about her days on campus, Devin, who stood offstage, felt someone sidle up next to him. Wearing a press pass around his neck, the young man who had somehow slipped past security wore a bright red afro and wire rimmed glasses.

"Mr. Simmons, I'm Editor of the Opinions section of the school newspaper and I just want to know one thing," said the student, whose press pass read Riley Moore. Realizing he had to move fast if he wanted to get a quote, Riley turned his phone recorder on before Devin could protest, and continued. "You identify as bisexual but you never accept invites to speak at LGBTQ+ events or pride rallies. You don't even really talk about legislation affecting our community. Are you ashamed of being part of it?"

Shocked by how forward the young reporter was being, Devin started to answer but was interrupted by Vanessa, who quickly swept in at Darlene's beckoning.

"Let's go, baby, April is about to call you," she said over the noise.

Devin gave a brief nod before taking her hand and looking back to Riley.

"I'm very proud of who I am, and I'm happy that so far during this campaign my ideas and experience have taken a front seat, and not my personal life."

At that moment he was called to the stage.

"Stick around for a little bit," said Devin, before excusing himself and joining Vanessa and April at the podium.

Devin gave his famous smile, waited for the applause to die down and delivered a speech that was so powerful it was replayed across news stations and featured in the morning paper. Riley's question encouraged Devin to take a personal approach, and he decided to speak about being a bisexual black man and how running a race to become a member of Congress had been difficult. He shared the challenges he'd faced so far and discussed the obstacles likely to come. Though he didn't talk about it often, Devin briefly told the room about the death threats he'd received, later assuring them that threats and intimidation would not deter him from winning in November. Reports of the speech quickly hit news channels, and Devin was recognized for his vulnerability, making him more relatable and beloved to the people of Maryland.

CHAPTER 13

NEW FRIENDS, OLD FRIENDS

"Hold the door!" called out Charles Welsh as he rushed to make the elevator. A hand reached out to stop the sliding doors and Welsh quickly glided in.

"Thank you," he muttered while pushing the button to the fourth floor. He remembered a time when he'd worked on one of the higher floors, but those days were long gone.

"Special Agent Welsh?" asked a woman in a tailor-made suit that fit her and her curves like a glove.

Not the friendliest person since his accident, and always short with words, Welsh started to grunt in the woman's direction until he looked up and realized who the voice belonged to. He was surprised to see Supervisory Special Agent Sandra Perry, who joined the FBI in the late 90s and was assigned to the Washington Field Office. During the course of her career she worked counterintelligence, public corruption, civil rights and violent crime.

Following her fallout with the bureau after the Thaddeus Simmons case, Agent Perry, or Sandra as her colleagues referred to her, had been reassigned to the Atlanta field office where she worked hard and redeemed herself. Now, having been named head of the FBI's new public corruption program, she was back at headquarters and in the bureau's good graces. She was a wonderful leader, and despite her naivete during the Simmons case, she had proven herself and had regained trust.

"Hello ma'am, it's great to have you back up north," Welsh said with a rare smile. "I'm surprised you remember my name."

"Of course, I make it my business to remember the best agents I've ever had the privilege to work with or know. I was sad to hear about your accident, the field lost a great agent."

Touched that she'd remembered some of his earlier accomplishments, when the elevator dinged, Welsh reluctantly began to exit.

"Thank you. It was great seeing you again Agent Perry."

Reaching into her laptop bag, Sandra pulled out a glossy business card.

"Just call me Sandra. Same to you, and if you ever need anything, please reach out. My cell is on the back."

Taking the card and placing it in his front pocket, for the first time in a long time, Welsh felt like he belonged. With a newfound purpose, he went to his desk, opened his computer and reviewed his calendar and emails for the day, but his mind couldn't focus on the work before him. Instead, it reverted back to his accident and his recent meeting with journalist, Ian Thompson.

Feelings of self-pity soon turned to anger as he thought about the man who'd put him in the wheelchair. Exiting out of his emails, he typed in the name that had haunted him for years, Regis Adams. As his cursor went over every article highlighting Adams, his anger grew. At that moment he knew he had a decision to make. Live in fear and shame or confront his past.

Sitting at his computer in his home office, Ian absently rubbed his beard as he stared at the blank screen before him, frustrated. He'd called all of his contacts, asking around about Regis Adams, and all he was met with were hang ups and people rushing him off the phone before he could even mention the man's full name. The vibrating phone on his desk took his attention off of the computer as he looked down at the caller ID and answered immediately.

"Hello," he said.

"Ian, it's Welsh. I'm in. I want us to get Regis Adams."

CHAPTER 14

JUST ANOTHER DAY

Sipping his coffee and reading the latest copy of *The Daily Sun,* Jacob smiled. Devin was on the front page of the paper, highlighted in an article about his speech at Morgan State University. His vulnerability and openness was shocking for a politician, and to everyone's relief he had been well received. People were well aware of his stance on civil and voting rights, but this time, at the encouragement of the young reporter named Riley Moore, he had spoken candidly about his plans for the LGBTQ+ community, including ideas to ensure the protection of members of the community from housing, financial, and employment discrimination. To further shock the public, he even spoke briefly about public corruption and white-collar crimes, something he rarely did.

"I will support legislation that will help prevent white collar crimes at the national, state and local levels," read Jacob. Devin never mentioned his father but the quote said it all. He did not condone what his father had been accused of and would not put up with it if elected. Looking up from the article, Jacob saw it was a little after noon. Hungry and wanting some air, he decided to grab some food from the corner deli. Using the phone in the conference room, he dialed his assistant.

"Hey, Celeste, hold my calls for an hour please, I'm making a run to Potbelly's," he said into the speaker phone. "Want anything?"

"Sir, you know I can go for you, it'll just take me fifteen minutes to run there and back."

Wanting to enjoy the nice weather and get out of the building, Jacob declined. Normally he would work through lunch but today he needed the fresh air that the outdoors offered.

Pocketing his wallet, he stepped outside. Maryland was so beautiful during the springtime, and it seemed like everyone thought the same thing as they crowded the streets. Taking in the views, Jacob didn't notice the man who walked up to him on his right.

"Jacob, hi, do you have a minute to talk?" asked an older man who was trying to catch up to Jacob's long strides.

Shit, Jacob thought when he saw that it was Ian Thompson, the journalist who'd been leaving messages on his answering machine and sending emails every two days. Instead of slowing down for the older man, who was clearly having a tough time keeping up with him, he increased his speed.

Not one to be easily dismissed, Ian started a slow jog, much to Jacob's surprise.

"What can I do for you?" Jacob asked, since it was clear his company wasn't leaving.

"I'm Ian Thompson with the *The Daily Sun*. I've tried calling your office..."

Ian knew he only had Jacob's attention for another minute or so, so he played all his cards.

"I think your friend, Thaddeus, was framed and killed. I don't think he really committed suicide and I think Regis Adams had something to do with it. Do you know anything about that?"

"I don't," Jacob said as he walked up the deli steps, hoping fear didn't shine in his eyes and that he appeared confident.

The problem was, fear did show, and Ian noticed the panicked look immediately. "Well, I've left many emails and messages for you with my contact information. If you think of anything. Anything at all. Call me and help me get to the bottom of everything."

Sending a quick nod to the reporter, Jacob turned and hurried into the deli, wishing he'd never taken this lunch break.

CHAPTER 15

ALL NIGHT LONG

It was May 28th, and for his thirtieth birthday, Julian invited more than 200 people to his home to celebrate. It had been a couple of months since Avery stormed out of his life, and despite Julian's attempts to talk to her, she refused to answer his calls. Now, he was back to living his bachelor life. Dating was never a problem for him, and women flocked to him like white on rice, especially when they found out how loaded he was.

Joining him to host his party was twenty-four-year-old Instagram model and influencer, Jade. After trying to get back in his good graces for weeks, Julian finally let her in. The two met on social media six months prior, and in spite of what he hoped was a temporary moment of insanity on her end during Avery's visit, their arrangement seemed to work. After a stern conversation with Julian, she had promised to never act out like that again. Julian reluctantly took her back and invited her to his birthday party as his date. She was a gorgeous arm-piece and completed his look perfectly for the night—black, rich and successful.

Julian was enjoying the steamy sex while Jade lavished in the financial benefits.

Guests began arriving around nine that evening, dressed in everything from Laquan Smith originals to Brandon Blackwood, and the air was filled with expensive scents. Business partners, friends, fraternity brothers, family and even a few celebrities all came together for the massive celebration, and they weren't disappointed. The pool area was filled with people enjoying the seventy-degree weather and sipping cocktails.

Vanessa arrived a couple of hours into the party, sans Devin who was at a fundraising gala. While she normally accompanied him to events where donors would be present, it was important to both of them that she attend Julian's birthday party, especially since Devin couldn't. Standing in the doorway, her eyes darted around, taking in all the festivities. This party was more lavish than she'd expected, but knowing Julian, she wasn't surprised.

"Damn, there's some fine ass men in this room," said Mikayla, her best friend, gesturing towards a group of men who stood together in the far corner of the room, talking.

"Yeah if you're looking for a good time," laughed Vanessa. "I think those guys play basketball so that tells you everything you need to know."

Even as Vanessa said this, she knew better. Those guys didn't stand a chance with Mikayla, who played men better than Lori Harvey. Since the day they met on the board of a charity event, Vanessa had watched Mikayla chew men up and spit them out more times than she could count. With four broken engagements she was the dream of many men, with her charm, beauty and smarts. She had a gift for drawing people in and making them feel special, plus, she was hilarious. On the flipside, she was indecisive and grew bored quickly. Following many failed relationships that she ultimately ended, Mikayla finally decided that she had no interest in having children or being married. Years earlier, when Vanessa asked if she ever wanted to settle down, Mikayla said with a straight face, "I'm having too much fun right now. If I had a man, he'd be getting cheated on, and my poor child would end up with abandonment issues. Ask me again when I'm like fifty."

Mikayla loved the life she lived and the freedom it allotted her. The only person she had to worry about was herself, and she thrived on the excitement that each day brought. This was why her job as a talent agent, was perfect. Not only was every day an adventure, but the high- profile people, as well as those she met in the entertainment industry, kept her engaged in her work. Vanessa was sure Mikayla's big personality would attract the attention of many people, men and women, before the end of the night.

People were always surprised to learn of her commitment to service and giving back. She earned a hefty living, and what she didn't spend or save, she donated to different causes, usually anonymously. That was what Vanessa loved most about her friend. She got to see the warm side of Mikayla, the intimate moments, and wished she'd share that side more often with others.

"You're right," Mikayla said, grinning. "I've had enough of athletes, they're too much for me."

Walking further into the party, Vanessa spotted Julian through the window, by the pool. "Come on, Mick, I see Julian out back."

Walking to the pool was a whole experience. Dancers were performing in enclosed cases surrounded by flickering lights. This was definitely Julian's style.

"Vanessa!" called Julian as soon as she appeared on the terrace.

He immediately placed his bottle on the table and walked towards his future sister-in-law and her friend. He was so drunk and high from the party he didn't notice Jade as she quickly stood up to walk with him towards the girls.

After spotting Mikayla as soon as she'd walked outside, Jade's claws immediately came out.

Drake's song, *Way 2 Sexy* started to play, and Julian stopped halfway to put on a show. Guests looked on and clapped with laughter as he gyrated his hips and humped the ground like he was a member of Pretty Ricky. Finally, the song was over and Julian reached over to hug Vanessa.

"Sis, it's my muthafucking birthday!"

Releasing Vanessa from his tight embrace, he looked over at Mikayla and smiled.

"Aww Mick, you came down from New York to celebrate with your boy!"

Laughing at his slurred words, Mikayla patted his shoulder.

"I wasn't about to miss this event, you throw the best parties."

"Ahemmmm," came a sound that took them away from the conversation.

Arms folded, Jade looked Mikayla up and down.

"Aren't you going to introduce me, baby?"

"Why? We don't go together." And with that, Julian left Jade standing alone as he led the two ladies to a cabana, reserved especially for them. Following behind him, Vanessa leaned over toward Mikayla.

"That girl is crazy, good thing she doesn't know you and Julian hooked up before."

Mikayla shook her head in agreement.

"I like Julian because he's a lot like me. I still think he should let me represent him, he has a big personality and a good following on social media. He was born for show business, not for crunching numbers. Anyway, we had our fun, now we're good friends. But it's something about that girl I'm nervous about. He needs to watch his back with that one."

Back in the house, Jacob was in the kitchen pouring himself another glass of scotch. This wasn't his kind of party, but he'd never missed a birthday and had wanted to stop by even if it was only for a short time. *After this drink, I'm heading out*, he thought to himself.

Jacob turned around to head back to Julian's entertainment room. Julian had the room prepared just for him, knowing he would want to sit down and be away from the craziness of the party. Jacob almost dropped his cup when he spotted a new face in the room.

"I hope I'm not interrupting your me-time."

Regis was sitting in one of the chairs facing the stadium-size television screen where Julian played video games or watched his sports programs.

"I figured this was the best time and place for us to talk right quick. Jacob, I thought we had an understanding."

Unsure where this was leading, Jacob remained quiet.

Regis reached into his coat jacket and pulled out his phone. For a few seconds he scrolled through the contents of his photo album until he stopped at the picture he wanted to show Jacob. Placing the cellphone before him, Jacob, annoyed at this surprise visit and nervous at the same time, glanced at the image with alarm. The photo showed him entering the deli last week with Ian Thompson. Even though the full exchange wasn't shown, this photo would have anyone thinking they knew each other.

"Regis, what the hell, you're having me followed?"

"Watch that bass in your voice when you talk to me and stop trying to deflect. Tell me, what did you and Mr. Thompson talk about?"

"Nothing," Jacob said in exasperation. "He's been reaching out to me for a while and I've been ignoring him. He came to my office and followed me at lunch time. I didn't tell him anything."

"What did he say to you, and don't leave shit out."

"He just said he was looking for more information on Thaddeus, that was it. It was a quick walk up the street, no longer than two minutes, tops," said Jacob, who intentionally left out Ian calling Regis out, by name.

"Yeah well, I don't believe you, Jacob, and you should know by now not to play with me."

Just as quickly as Regis appeared at the party, he was gone.

CHAPTER 16

BRAKE LIGHT

The day after Julian's birthday party, Devin was up and moving while Vanessa was half awake, nursing a pounding headache. The party was a great time and she'd had more glasses of wine than she'd anticipated.

Barely raising her head in Devin's direction, she released a soft moan.

"Baby, my head is killing me."

"You brought down the house last night, hunh?" said Devin with laughter in his eyes. "You came in here falling over last night, knocking everything over in the bathroom. Do you remember grabbing my junk when you laid down? You got me excited just to fall asleep on me."

"Shut up and grab me some ibuprofen out the cabinet," she growled.

Devin stopped unpacking his suitcase from his trip the previous day and went to find the medicine. He knew from experience that Vanessa was a terror when she was hungry, the first two days of her period, and when she didn't feel well, and he didn't want to be on the receiving end of her rage.

"There's only Advil in here."

"I want Ibuprofen, Devin!"

Jumping at the high-pitched screech in her voice, Devin bit his tongue and grabbed his car keys.

"I'll be back."

It was the weekend, which meant Ms. Ruby was off and they were on their own. Normally, Vanessa started her Saturdays off with a nice brunch, but it was clear that no cooking would be happening that day. Instead of having the medicine delivered, Devin decided a drive to the store would be faster.

Before taking off, Devin pulled up GrubSpot and ordered breakfast for delivery then notified the guard gate that someone would be bringing food within the hour. The local grocery store was a quick 10-minute drive from his house in Howard County, and even though he usually had a 24-hour security detail with him, Devin insisted he drive alone and security stay behind. It was rare for Devin to drive his own car, and on the few occasions he was able to spend alone in his Porsche, he relished it. Music pumped through the sound system as he sped well over the 60-mph speed limit, dodging local traffic.

Approaching a red light midway to his final stop, Devin released the gas pedal and pressed the brake to stop. Pressing down on the brake pedal to no avail, Devin panicked when he realized he couldn't come to a stop. A scream rang out, and within moments, he lay unconscious, with his head on the wheel and onlookers reaching for their phones to either record the incident or call for an ambulance.

The light illuminated the room, and a hand covered in needles reached up to shield his eyes. With blurry vision, Devin couldn't make out where he was, until he heard a beeping noise and noticed the familiar smell of a hospital. Instinctively, he began sitting up, but a throbbing ache in his back stopped him.

"Devin, baby, just relax," said Vanessa, who sounded like she was far away. After calling for a nurse, she turned back to her fiancé and massaged his right arm.

"Vanessa, what the fuck is going on?" asked Devin faintly.

"You've been out for almost a full day. Do you remember being in a car accident?"

Before he could answer, a nurse bounded into the hospital suite and asked Vanessa to step to the side as she checked his vitals. Closing his eyes, his mind raced back to the moments before his accident. He'd driven through an intersection and had hit a car. He remembered glass shattering in all directions and paramedics lifting him into the stretcher. That was the last memory he had. He closed his eyes, willing himself to remember more, but he couldn't.

"Mr. Simmons, you are very lucky. You were in a three-car collision yesterday. You've been in a coma for seventeen hours. Sir, we are very happy to see you awake."

"What about the other people involved, are they okay?"

The room fell silent before Vanessa suggested they talk about that later.

"No, tell me."

Reaching for his hand, she gently caressed his palm.

"There were three others. One sustained a minor injury and the other two are in critical condition. A mother and her twelve-year-old son got the worst of it."

Moving his hand away from hers, Devin let out a soft moan. Once the nurse on duty did a final check to make sure Devin was out of the woods, she walked out just as Uncle Jacob, who'd been in the waiting area with Julian, Ms. Ruby and Darlene, walked in. Surprised to see that Devin was up, he rushed to his side.

"Nephew, I haven't had a scare like this in a long time, I'm happy you're okay," said Jacob, his hand on Devin's shoulder. Jacob took his role of playing surrogate father to Devin and Julian seriously and was upset when he'd learned of the accident.

"I'm happy too, Unc, I just hope that lady and her son pull through. I don't know what happened. I remember coming to the red light and trying to stop, but my brakes gave out on me. Y'all know me, I drive a little fast but I'm never reckless."

Jacob's eyes narrowed as he thought about what Devin was saying. Something wasn't right.

"I'll look into it, Devin, we'll get the car looked at today. You just take it easy and try to relax. I'll let everyone in the waiting room know you're up so they can come in to visit, and I'll be back to check on you after I see what's going on with your car."

"Thank you, Unc," said Devin in a dry tone.

Noticing the scratchiness in his voice, Vanessa grabbed a cup of water, placing the straw in his mouth for him to sip from.

On his way to the parking garage, Jacob stopped and looked around. He felt someone watching him. Shaking off the paranoia, Jacob continued on towards his car and got settled in the front seat. Then he noticed a note nestled inside the cup holder. Looking around frantically, wondering how someone had been able to get inside his locked car, he reached for the handgun he kept in a secret compartment before looking down to read the note:

REMEMBER, THIS ISN'T A GAME YOU WANT TO PLAY.

Balling up the note and placing his gun back in its place, Jacob sat rigidly upright in his seat as blood rushed to his head. Starting his car, he raced out of the garage, seeing red. He couldn't do anything about what happened to Thaddeus, but Jacob would be damned if anything happened to either of his late friend's sons. For years he had been playing offense, it was time to go on the defense, and he knew the first play he wanted to make.

CHAPTER 17

BIG NEWS

The blaring sound from Julian's phone pulled Devin's attention away from his brother. Julian had been by Devin's side since he was released from the hospital five days ago. Now, Devin was back at home and in his own bed. The brothers were very close, and Julian was grateful his brother was alive and doing well. Surprised that the caller was Avery, he excused himself and stepped out of the room to answer the call.

"Avery?"

"Hey, Julian," said the voice on the other end of the line.

Usually upbeat and happy, Julian could tell immediately that something was wrong.

"Baby, have you been crying?"

Julian knew that Avery hated when he called her pet names, but he couldn't help it. She brought out the loving side of him. Barely able to make a sentence, Avery managed to blurt out, "I'm pregnant!"

Dropping the phone to his side, Julian didn't know

whether to be happy or concerned. A part of him was pleased to be having a baby with the girl of his dreams, but he couldn't help but feel sad for Avery, who sounded like her world was closing in. All of a sudden, a thought came to him.

"And it's mine?" he asked softly.

Avery's cries increased as she thought about the mess she was in. "Yes, Julian, it's yours," she said through tears.

"I'll catch the red eye tonight and will be in Los Angeles by the morning."

With that, the call disconnected. Julian went back to tell Devin, who lay barely awake, that there was an emergency but he would call later to check on him. Devin, in a fog from all the meds he'd been taking, grunted before closing his eyes to go back to sleep.

Vanessa, who was nearby, could tell something was up. She told Julian to be careful as she walked him to the door. Stopping at home briefly to pack a bag, he jetted for the airport, his mind clouded with thoughts of a baby.

Touching down in Los Angeles, Julian looked out the window and shook his head. He never understood the hype about L.A., but he knew Avery loved it. On the instructions of the flight attendant, he unbuckled his seat belt, stood up from his first-class seat, reached for his overhead bag and prepared to exit the plane. Almost as soon as he stepped off the plane he felt a graze on his arm. Looking up, the flight attendant who'd been flirting with him the entire flight, held out a piece of paper with a number scrawled on it.

The passengers behind Julian impatiently waited for

him to move on. For a second, Julian thought about taking her digits, until a picture of Avery came to mind. Sending the stewardess a small smile but shaking his head no, he turned around and headed up the jet-bridge.

After sitting in traffic, he eventually steered his rental car into the driveaway of a nice home in the Woodland Hills. Avery was an entertainment lawyer and made a great living. Unlike Julian, she came from humble beginnings.

Her mother was a retired elementary school teacher who'd worked in the Philadelphia school district for a quarter of a century. If it weren't for the increase of violence in schools, she would have happily waited another five years to retire, but at sixty, something told her it was time. Avery's dad owned a small barbershop in Philly, and was well-known in the community from his younger days as a boxer. Avery was a scholarship kid who maintained a 4.0 GPA from the time she graduated high school through her time at the University of Pennsylvania Carey Law School. She'd had a solid upbringing and worked hard to be able to afford her own home in L.A.

Before he could knock on the door, it swung open, with Avery standing in the doorframe looking fragile and tired. Leading Julian to the chaise, she sat on the couch. Determined to get everything out in the open, Avery brought her hands together and held them on her lap.

"Julian, this isn't my first baby," she quivered. "I got pregnant back when we were together at school."

Julian could tell she was struggling to look him in the eye, and as the words registered, he became tense.

"I was pregnant when that girl jumped on me when I was walking through campus."

As she spoke, that day in question popped into Julian's mind. He could still remember Avery calling him from the hospital, upset. Brigette, a girl from Temple he'd been seeing on the side, came to campus to confront Avery after seeing her name on his phone the night before. A quick search on Facebook helped her locate Avery, and she decided to sit outside the law school building all morning in hopes of spotting the woman who clearly had Julian's heart.

Passing through campus, Avery had felt someone approach her from behind and swung around to see who it was. Instead of talking, Brigette took a swing at Avery, knocking her to the ground before jumping on top of her. It took four students to pull the women apart, and by that time the campus police had arrived. Brigette was taken to jail, and a bleeding Avery was sent to the local hospital. It was there that Avery found out she was eleven weeks pregnant. That day Avery did two things. First, she called Julian to break up with him, then she scheduled an abortion. There was no way she could bring a baby into the world with a man who couldn't be trusted. That day changed her life forever. The more she talked, the more things started to make sense.

"Avery, I'm so sorry you went through all that alone. You should have been able to come to me, but I understand why you didn't. I wasn't the man you needed me to be, and with what happened recently, during your visit, maybe I'm still not."

After hours of talking, Avery and Julian both felt like a load had been lifted off of them, and they both retired for a nap. Julian was still tired from the long flight, and in her first trimester, Avery was feeling exhausted. Days went by, and after making sure his brother was healing well, Julian decided to stay in L.A. and spend a much-needed week with Avery.

CHAPTER 18

THE MEETUP

Ian Thompson walked into the lavish hotel lobby and went straight to the elevator. Looking down at the piece of paper that listed the room number, he got off on the appropriate floor and gave the door a soft knock. Within seconds, the door swung open, and a man who looked like the weight of the world rested on his shoulders was standing there.

"Hurry inside," he barked.

Aware of the risk his subject was taking, Ian quickly stepped inside, closing the door behind him. Noticing the handgun resting on Jacob's hip, Ian knew whatever the man had to say, had to be a game changer.

"You coming up to me on the street put a target on my back," Jacob started, looking Ian angrily in the eye. "And you put Devin in danger. Because of you, he almost died!" he continued, his voice rising in anger. Balling his fist, Ian feared that Jacob could strike him at any moment.

When Jacob learned that Devin's faulty brakes had

been the cause of his nephew's accident, he had the vehicle inspected. As he'd thought, the car had been rigged and the note in his cup holder convinced him that Regis was behind the accident. A day later, Jacob bought and used a burner phone to get in contact with Ian. Keeping their communication short, he'd requested a meeting at a hotel, and sent the room number to Ian, who'd learned of Devin's accident and knew this meeting might be tied to it. To turn the attention off of himself, Ian directed Jacob's focus back to the crash.

"The accident was planned, wasn't it?" Ian asked.

Thoughts of Regis came into Jacob's mind, and he growled in response.

"Go ahead, tell me," Ian coaxed.

Taking his steely eyes off of Ian, Jacob took a seat on the couch and looked out the window, trying to get his emotions under control.

Ian sat on a nearby chair and waited for Jacob to speak.

"Regis caused the accident," he began. "It was his way of threatening me to keep my mouth shut about what really happened to Thaddeus."

"—and what really happened?"

Letting out a loud sigh, Jacob squeezed his eyes shut and recalled the events leading up to, and after, his late friend's arrest.

"The night before the raid, Thaddeus called me and said there was something he needed to talk to me about. He wasn't comfortable speaking over the phone and suggested we talk about it at work the next day. He sounded paranoid, almost like he was being watched. I never found out what was wrong, because the next day the feds came and took him away."

Rubbing his eyes, Jacob took a second to gather his thoughts.

"I finally got to visit and speak with him when he was locked up. The night before his so-called suicide, we sat down and he kept looking around, like the guards or someone was after him. In a low whisper, he said, *Friday*."

Confused about what the day of the week or perhaps a reference to a black movie had to do with anything, Ian sat back and waited for Jacob to explain.

For a second, Jacob had a small smile on his face. His days as a plebe at the Naval Academy were always fun to talk about.

"One weekend during spring semester of our freshman year of college Thaddeus and I decided to go to a house party in Baltimore. It was my idea. A girl I knew from high school, whom I'd always wanted to get with, was throwing it, so I had to be there. There weren't a lot of black people in Annapolis, and we weren't allowed to have cars on campus as freshmen, so I called a friend of mine to come pick us up. Thaddeus and I snuck out after curfew, along with Timothy Reynolds, another plebe at the Academy, and headed to what we thought would be a great party."

"Man, I can't wait to meet your old friends," said Timothy from the backseat.

Rolling his eyes, Jacob once again wondered how he'd let the white boy sucker him into letting him come. Pulling up to the party, it was packed. Spilling out of the house, people danced wherever they were to the music pumping from the stereo. Jumping out of the car, Timothy was ready for a good time.

"Ohhhh yeah, here we go!"

Pulling him to the side, Jacob spoke through clenched teeth.

"You're already white, don't bring more attention to yourself. Just be cool."

"I'm cool," said Timothy, placing his hands in his front pockets, trying to look less excited.

Thaddeus and Jacob made eye contact, and silently prayed there would be no issues that night. For an hour, it was smooth sailing. Nina, Jacob's crush from high-school, grinded on him to New Edition's, *Can You Stand the Rain*, and both Timothy and Thaddeus were talking to a couple of girls by the punch bowl.

The boys were having a good time, until a barrage of red, white and blue lights glared through the windows of the row house. The police had arrived just in time for the turned-up portion of the evening. After the slow jams came the gangster rap, and the crowd was on fire.

Loud noises coming from outside made the deejay lower the volume so they could hear what was going on. Officers carrying batons demanded that everyone disperse or they'd be arrested. No one had called to complain about the noise, so it was clear the officers were there on their own to intimidate the partiers.

Thaddeus turned to his classmates, motioning for them to follow him through the backdoor and away from the house. Jacob obliged, but Timothy had other plans. By the time Jacob noticed Timothy walking in the opposite direction, it was too late. Marching towards an officer who was ushering people out the door, Timothy lifted his arms and screamed, "Fuck the police," a reference to NWA's hit song at the time. He expected people to join in, but no one did."

Timothy screamed it again, and this time threw a fold-up chair that was sitting next to him towards no one in particular, for emphasis. Everyone at the party turned their attention to him in shock. Before he could yell it again, nervous laughter filled the place. Grabbing him, the officer closest to Timothy, handcuffed and pushed him outside towards the squad car."

Jacob smiled at the memory and so did Ian.

"It was a Friday so Timothy had to spend the weekend in jail," laughed Jacob. "Afterwards he swore he had more street cred." For a second Jacob stopped talking and briefly wondered what Timothy was up to now. "Anyway, after that, me and Thaddeus decided to use *Friday* as our code word whenever we were in trouble. This was the first time either of us needed to use it, but I immediately knew to check his safe. We both had safes in our homes, and access to each other's."

Jacob went on to detail his findings. In addition to a letter highlighting his involvement with Regis and Congressman Rucker, there was a recording device containing several conversations between Thaddeus and Regis.

"It was like his insurance policy in case anything happened to him. In one recording Thaddeus shared that Tara, his assistant, had been put in place to spy on him by the FBI. Once the feds had enough on Thaddeus, they approached him and he was put in place to spy on Regis, or go to jail for corruption. Regis has long been suspected of being a major player in a notorious bribery ring, and the FBI was ready to take down everyone involved. To protect his family and avoid prison time, Thaddeus chose to go against Regis.

The night I found out all of this, I got a call from Brenda. I was too late. Thaddeus had been found hanging from a makeshift rope in his cell. I refused to believe he killed himself. From the notes Thaddeus had taken, something told me that this was all Regis's doing. I'm not sure what really happened with Congressman Rucker, but I know Thaddeus didn't do that either. Outside of his time in the military during war, he wasn't capable of killing anyone, plus he was working with the FBI, so why would he kill someone if he had such a sweet deal with them? Before Thaddeus could expose Regis, Regis had him framed and killed. I just know it."

Jacob had always had a bad feeling about Regis. The day Thaddeus introduced the two men, Jacob knew the man was bad news, but all Thaddeus cared about was money and power, even if it meant getting in bed with one of D.C.'s most powerful but dangerous players.

"Regis doesn't know I know all of this, but he's always suspected I was privy to something. Over the years, he's always made comments and threats. One day he said something that made me sit up in my seat. About a year after Thaddeus died, he popped up at Julian's homecoming football game. He would check in on the boys occasionally. I think he was doing it out of guilt. He always said Thaddeus was like a younger brother to him, so he felt the need to be there for the boys when he could. Anyway, somewhere during half-time the subject of the anniversary of Thaddeus's death came up. All I said was that I still didn't believe he killed himself, and Regis looked me in the eye and said it would be best if I kept my opinions to myself. Then, looking out to the football field where Julian played, he said, "The tongue is a powerful tool, it can get people killed."

Ian looked on with his mouth gaped open, partly from what was being shared and also due to how open Jacob was being.

"You've held on to all of this, this whole time? You haven't told a soul?"

Ian couldn't imagine holding on to this heavy load of information for that long, especially details that could single handedly save his friend's legacy.

"I don't have kids of my own, those boys are like mine. And Brenda…"

His voice trailed off for a second. "Look, I promised Thaddeus I would look out for them, so yeah I kept my mouth shut. Even with Regis in their lives, helping out on Devin's campaign, I figured they were safe. But now, I know they're not."

Looking out the window at nothing in particular, images of seeing Devin in the hospital bed clouded his vision and infuriated him all over again.

"Agent Welsh is working on re-opening this case," said Ian, bringing him back to the present.

"Tell him I'm in. But the real person y'all need to talk to is Brittany Garcia."

"The girl who was with Congressman Rucker the night he was killed? She's in the wind."

"Yes, I'm pretty sure Regis paid her to lie. Remember that lawyer she had? There's no way she could have afforded him on her own. Then afterwards it's like she just disappeared. But Ian? Regis won't go down without a fight. We both know the power he holds around here. I hope you and Welsh have a solid plan."

For the first time since diving back into the story, Ian was unsure that they did, or if any of them would live to see justice served.

CHAPTER 19

AFTERMATH

A full week had passed since the accident, and Devin was finally able to move around the house on his own. Though he was still a bit mopey, his spirits were lifted after learning that the mother and son from the accident would be okay. They were still in bad shape, but were expected to make a full recovery. Devin wanted to visit them in the hospital, or at least send flowers, but Darlene was adamant that they not reach out. A lawsuit was surely coming, and reporters were tearing Devin up in the press. Fake news floated around that he was drunk during the accident, and some even claimed the twelve-year-old boy was dead, which was a complete lie.

"Devin, we need to make a statement to the press, these stories are getting out of control. Now that those two have pulled through, it's time we say something."

Darlene was irritating the shit out of Devin. His head pounded every time she opened her mouth. He and several others were almost killed, and this is what she wanted to talk about? Making a statement?

Sighing at his obvious disdain for the conversation, Darlene continued. "Devin, there's something else." Reaching for the remote that lay on the table, she flicked on the television that had been off since the accident, and turned to CNN.

"Darlene, I told you I don't want to hear what they're saying. It's all lies!"

"Well, you're going to watch this. I need you to see what's being put out there."

Turning the corner into the living room, Vanessa stopped and gasped as a montage of footage taken of Devin's mother spilled across the television.

"They're saying you were drunk, Devin! And they've obtained film of your mother to make their point."

"How'd they even get this? Some of this was filmed at the party she just threw for him, so who would share this with the news?" asked Vanessa in disgust.

"My guess is Senator Brennan's team. They've been on edge since Devin announced he was running. They thought this was going to be a smooth re-election for him, but we've been winning over voters these last few months. It has to be them."

Devin was unconvinced that this was the Senator's doing. There were two seats to be filled, and Brennan had a good chance of reclaiming his seat this election cycle.

"My toxicology screen came back clean," said Devin as he watched the footage of his mother.

"And we released that information to the public, but you know people prefer the fake over the real," said Darlene.

Devin looked down and fidgeted with the handle of his

coffee cup, before turning to Vanessa.

"How's my mother doing?"

"Better, Devin, she's been clean for three months now."

"Well," Devin said, "whip up a statement for me, Darlene. And Vanessa, book us some flights to go and see my mother in Houston. I have to see this for myself. I'll know when I look at her if she's really been sober."

Without another word, he sat his mug on the table and slowly walked back to his room.

CHAPTER 20

PARENT'S NIGHT OUT

Five days had gone by and Julian was still in Los Angeles. After checking to make sure Devin was recovering well, he decided that time away from work, with Avery, was needed. He went to a doctor appointment with her, cooked his famous dishes and fixed things around the house that she hadn't gotten around to dealing with.

On Saturday morning, Avery looked on as Julian tinkered around with the door to the guest bedroom. He claimed the door wasn't shutting properly, but Avery suspected he was trying to make up for the times he had cheated and left her hanging.

"Yeah, I think I need to go to the hardware store to pick up some things for this," he said out loud.

"Julian, the door is fine. Aren't you tired of doing all this maintenance work?"

"I live across the country. I need to make sure everything is in place so you're comfortable until I come back next month."

"I'm pretty sure I can go a month with things as they are," laughed Avery. "We've been cooped up in this house all week, talking and working, can't we do something fun?"

Noticing the sparkle in her eye, he almost forgot how much of an adventurer she was. When she said fun, she meant doing things like sky diving, snorkeling, or bungee jumping.

"Hell no, baby, we're not jumping off of a building today, you're pregnant."

"No shit, Sherlock, I was thinking of something like the beach. It's nice out, let's go."

Julian thought for a second, and had an idea. "Cool, let's go tonight, when the sun goes down a little."

The two spent the day in the house, cuddling and sleeping. Eight o'clock rolled around, and as Julian approached the Santa Monica State Beach, Avery looked out to the sunset.

"This is beautiful," she said.

Finding a spot right off the boardwalk, facing the beach, Julian, placed the car in park. When Avery went to grab her things, he told her to stop and look up to the sky.

At that moment, a small plane flew across with a banner that read, *Avery, I love you.*

It was then that she noticed the table in front of her on a platform on the sand. Squealing with joy, she reached over to kiss Julian before hopping out of the car and running towards the set-up. That was Avery. So excited that she didn't even give Julian time to properly open her door and escort her to the table. Amused, Julian gathered up their beach belongings and followed the woman of his dreams.

Almost as soon as Avery mentioned going to the beach,

he had messaged his assistant Donna to plan a romantic night for Avery. As always, even from thousands of miles away, Donna, did her thing and organized a dinner through a local catering business with some of Avery's favorites. It was his final night with her before he had to head back home for work, and he wanted it to be special.

Dinner included lobster, oysters and steak. After what seemed like hours of laughing and stuffing themselves with good food, they leaned back in their chairs. Avery gazed out to the water while Julian gazed at her. Seconds went by until he broke the silence.

"Avery, I know this might not be the right time, but I have to say it," he said, then paused in hesitation.

Since the initial conversation they'd had when he first arrived in L.A. they hadn't had any more serious conversations, but this sounded important. Waiting for him to finish, she was interested to hear what he was going to say.

"I mean it, I love you, girl. Always have. If it's okay with you, I'd like for us to try again."

As sweet as that sounded, Avery fought not to roll her eyes. She knew he loved her, but could he really commit?

"Julian, just because I'm pregnant doesn't mean we should be together. And you live all the way on the east coast, let's be real here."

What she really wanted to say was 'boy please,' but she resisted the urge to crush his dreams, so she remained silent. Instead, the smirk she gave told Julian she wasn't buying what he was selling, and he could understand why.

"How about I show you? I know I've talked a lot before, but this time I'm going to show you."

Nodding her head slowly, Avery stood up, throwing her

dress over her head. Standing naked with her feet digging into the sand, she shared a smile before racing to the water.

Julian remained seated, unsure of what was happening.

"Get up! We're skinny dipping!"

Laughing, Julian delighted in her spontaneity. He never knew what he was going to get when he was with her, and that was what he loved the most. Taking off his clothes, he threw everything on the ground and took off after Avery Jones.

CHAPTER 21

H-TOWN

Vanessa's sister, Taryn, was an eclectic soul. True to her southern roots, she had no plans of ever moving from Houston, but as a celebrity stylist she got to travel all across the world to dress celebs and dignitaries. Most coveted for her role as one of Solange and Erykah Badu's stylists, she was considered both current and hip. She enjoyed making statements on the red carpet with her looks and was often interviewed by fashion correspondents. She made monthly trips to New York and was always seen sitting front row at different fashion shows in Milan and Paris. Though she had an apartment in New York, she always felt more comfortable in Houston. It was a no-brainer for her to help with Vanessa's dream wedding dress and bridal party looks, so when Vanessa and Devin's last-minute trip to check on Devin's mother came up, the sisters decided to use the time to do some planning and shopping.

Dressed entirely in black and wearing a vibrant turban, Taryn stood out to Vanessa and Devin as they exited the plane.

"Taryn!" cried an excited Vanessa as she ran up to her sister. "How'd you even get to the gate? I thought you'd be outside waiting in the pick-up lane."

"You're finally home! I don't even remember the last time you came for a visit!"

The two talked over each other, asking questions and answering at the same time while rocking one another in their arms. The sisters were a force when they were together. Taryn had a confidence that brightened every room, similar to that of her sister's, and an aura that attracted people from all walks of life. Her presence alone was peaceful and Zen. Taryn observed her younger sister, who looked as beautiful as ever, but noted sadness in her eyes. Finally, Devin interrupted the reunion.

"Come on, it's my turn now."

Taryn released her sister, deciding to savor the moment and choosing to ignore her concerns for the time being. Kissing Vanessa's cheek, she moved towards Devin for a hug. She really liked Devin for Vanessa, and had liked him since the day they met. Taryn valued authenticity and had a gift for discernment. She studied energy, the elements, and could always tell a lot about a person based on the energy they emitted when she was in their presence. Devin's presence told her that he was a good person, who had honorable intentions. The trio walked outside to Taryn's car.

"Where's my nephew?" Vanessa asked, referring to her sister's six-year-old son, Trey.

"Mom's at my house watching him. I put him to bed before I left. This was a late flight and he has school tomorrow. He was so mad at me but I promised him he'd have some time with you," smiled Taryn.

After the luggage was loaded they started the drive from George Bush Intercontinental Airport to their parents' house in The Woodlands. Since their parents had a hard time driving at night they had asked Taryn to pick up Vanessa and Devin. Every time they came for a visit, Vanessa's family insisted they use a family car instead of renting one, so they would pick out one of her parents' spare cars to use for the weekend once they made it to the house. Devin always liked coming to Houston, the southern hospitality was top tier and he loved Vanessa's family. His own family was boring compared to hers, which was larger in number and had more fun. Devin's family was more structured and by the book, so coming to Houston was always a treat.

"How's my boy, Kevin?" asked Devin.

The look on Taryn's face made him regret asking.

"You didn't tell him?" Taryn asked, looking briefly in the rearview mirror at Vanessa, who was sitting in the back.

"Figured you would when you were ready to share with everyone."

"We've been separated for about a month now."

At that, Taryn decided to switch the subject to something more exciting.

"Vanessa, look in that bag sitting next to you."

Ruffling through it, Vanessa's eyes lit up like lights on a Christmas tree. Whipping out a box full of six beignets from her favorite place in New Orleans, Café du Monde, she opened it and began stuffing one in her mouth.

"You do love me," she said as sugar fell off her mouth.

Taryn had returned from New Orleans the day before, and on her way back to Houston she had picked the treats up for Vanessa's visit. Shaking her head, Taryn couldn't believe her sister, who was such a lover of sweets, could keep her weight down to the 135 pounds that she was. She ate like a Houston Texans linebacker!

Reaching the street that their family had lived on since they were kids, Taryn cut the engine. They got out and approached the front. Before they reached the top step, the door swung open, followed by the screen.

"Well, it's about time y'all made it. You didn't run over anybody on the way here, like you did that mom and her child, did you?"

"Daddy, don't start with the jokes, especially the ones said in bad taste," said Vanessa as she reached out for a hug.

"Oh, baby you know I'm just messing with him. I can say 'him' right? Or have you been using pronouns like these kids been doing nowadays?"

Devin wasn't in the mood for Vanessa's ignorant ass daddy today.

"*Him* is fine, Calvin," he said as he pushed past Vanessa's father with their suitcases. His father-in-law-to-be had been a pain in the ass since the day they met. He was the complete opposite of Vanessa's mother, Celeste, who was the kindest woman Devin had ever met. She was a regular volunteer at the women's shelter and was heavily involved in her church, traits she'd gotten from her late father, Bishop Isaiah Barrett and had passed down to Vanessa. Celeste was such a prize, and a sweet person, that when she brought Calvin Covington home for the first time in the 80s, everyone was confused.

Calvin complained about all the issues happening around the world, never offering up solutions, whereas Celeste was active in the community and enjoyed working to solve the world's problems. Through all of their differences, they'd been together for three decades and were still going strong. Even still, Calvin was an acquired taste and not a lot of people recognized the good in him, as Celeste did.

Devin didn't like Calvin, who had a dry sense of humor and always had a rude comment to share. He was negative and a nuisance to be around. The icing on the cake had come shortly following his and Vanessa's engagement.

On their way back from Mexico, where Devin had proposed to Vanessa, the couple stopped in Houston to share the good news with her family. Sitting around a table for six at Pappadeaux, Vanessa extended her hand to show everyone at the table the glistening light from her diamond ring. No one was surprised. The pair had been dating for a little more than two years and had been talking marriage. Taryn and her mother oohed and ahhed, Kevin, Taryn's husband, congratulated them both, while Calvin remained quiet and stoic. No one noticed his quiet demeanor, and the excited chatter continued among the group until the food arrived and they bowed their heads for grace, with Calvin leading the prayer.

"Lord Jesus, thank you for this meal and for my daughters Taryn and Vanessa. Please cover them, as one lets her husband sleep around on her and the other is marrying a faggot—"

Before he could finish, Kevin, who was closest to his father-in-law, tackled the older man to the floor, swinging on top of him madly. Devin, always conscious of his environment and his image when in public, seethed quietly before jumping up to help the staff separate the two men, but it took all the patience he could muster not to take a swing on Vanessa's daddy, too. What was most confusing was the fact that Calvin had given Devin his blessing before the proposal. That was Calvin, wishy-washy and always the one to go for shock value. Seven months later, here they were, back for another visit.

"Well he's a little testy today," said Calvin to his daughters.

"Dad, he's been through a lot lately. Can you ease up on the jokes and not talk about his accident? We just want a peaceful weekend, please."

With a fake salute, he grinned and threw his arm around his youngest daughter.

"Well, I'm going to head home," said Taryn. "Mom is staying the night with me, but she'll be back here in the morning. Be good until she gets back here, Daddy."

"Why do y'all always think I'm up to something? I mind my business. I didn't even bring up Devin's mama yet!"

CHAPTER 22

THE PERFECT DRESS

"Okay Sis, I know you brought your wedding binder with you. Let's find your perfect dress."

The sisters sat around their parents' kitchen table, something they'd been doing since they were kids. It was where they came together for relationship advice, gossip, business talk and now, it was their meeting location for wedding dress discussions. With so much on her mind lately, thoughts of her dream dress made Vanessa smile, and she was excited to find the perfect look. Pulling out her portfolio, Vanessa began showing Taryn all the styles she loved. The two hatched a plan, and then Vanessa went to find Devin before leaving the house for what was sure to be an all-day mission.

"I can't believe you're leaving me here, with him," mumbled Devin when he learned that Vanessa would be out all day.

"Mom is back from Taryn's now, she'll keep you both in your corners. Try to ignore him, babe, you know he loves getting under your skin. Don't let him."

The car ride was spent discussing style and fit. It had been a while since they'd seen each other due to fluctuating work schedules on both parts, but the sisters, as close as they were, seemed to pick up right where they left off. The morning was a whirlwind as the girls met with four different black local designers in hopes of selecting one to design Vanessa's dress.

Finally, they retreated to one of their favorite lunch spots by the Galleria, Peli Peli. Cocktails began flowing and conversation was effortless as they talked about Taryn's latest trip to Milan. Finally, after a pregnant pause the discussion turned to Vanessa.

"Vanessa, whatsup with you? I can tell something is wrong."

With an eyebrow raised, Vanessa raised her glass to take another sip of her margarita before answering.

"Remember when I first told you about Regis? Devin's mentor?"

"Yeah, what about him? I remember you told me his energy was a little off."

"Well Devin thinks he walks on water, but I know there's something shady about him. Before Devin's accident I saw him at Julian's birthday party the night before, and it was weird."

Vanessa took a second to think back to the night of the party.

After sitting outside at Julian's party for a bit, she had headed inside to use the restroom. Passing by Julian's man-cave, she saw the door was slightly ajar, and Vanessa could make out Jacob and Regis's voices. First, she heard Jacob talking.

"He just said he was looking for more information on Thaddeus, that was it."

Pausing at the mention of her fiancé's father, she keyed in further.

"Yeah well, I don't believe you, Jacob," said Regis, but she couldn't make out the rest.

Now, turning to Taryn, Vanessa said, "I could tell he was threatening Jacob over information about Thaddeus. It was just off, Taryn, and all this was before Devin's accident. Something isn't right, but I don't know where to start. It's well known that Regis has been involved in a lot of powerful, but dark, circles. I just hope he has nothing but good intentions with Devin and this campaign. All I know is that I'm going crazy on this campaign trail, being away from my charity work, and now I feel like some dark shit is going down."

"And you don't want to tell Devin any of this?"

"How can I? The man just survived a bad accident and now he's here checking up on his mother. I think I'll do some research on my own before I bring my suspicions to him. Regis has brought the team a lot of money, maybe I should double check and make sure it's all legit and done by the book."

Grabbing her sister's hand, which rested on the table, Taryn squeezed it.

"That's a good place to start. Don't let this eat you up,

you're made for this. Granddaddy prepared you."

Thinking about their grandfather made Vanessa smile.

"Forever Papa's girls," they said in unison, reciting a line their grandfather would say to them. High-fiving each other, the day had gone well.

CHAPTER 23

LONG TIME COMING

When the sisters returned to their parents' house, they were surprised to see the front door open and suitcases sitting by the driveway, with Celeste flailing her arms in the air, yelling at someone standing behind the door. Almost as soon as Taryn placed her car in park, Devin flew through the open door. One look at how firmly he was clasping his duffel bag was a sign that he was furious. Following him out the door was Calvin. Vanessa made a full sprint to the door when she realized something bad must have happened between her fiancé and her father.

"Hey babe," Devin said in a calm but chilly voice. "I had my team book us at a hotel. I'm not putting up with your daddy, that ole wayward nigga is disrespectful and crazy."

And with that, Devin began loading their bags into the car that Vanessa's mother lent them for their visit. Mouth open, Vanessa was speechless. Devin had never been a fan of her dad, but he had never said anything outright mean or disrespectful about him to her face, until now. Knowing she wouldn't get anything more from Devin, she turned her attention to her mother, while Calvin went back in the house, shutting the door and leaving everyone out front. Wringing her hands on the front of her dress, Celeste was at a loss for words.

"It seemed like everything was going fine, but I guess things did kind of change when—"

"When what, Mom?" asked Taryn, who crossed the driveway to join her mother and sister.

"Well, I was telling Devin about all the new developments happening around Houston. He mentioned looking for a place here for him and Vanessa, especially if his mother decided to stay in town. Your father said, 'The east coast got tired of your mama's ole drunk ass so you want to bring her here?'"

"Oh no," Vanessa moaned. Hugging her mother, she turned and got into the car with a waiting Devin.

The next morning, they made the two-hour drive to Galveston, where Brenda was staying with Vanessa's cousin, Tommy, as she recovered. The evening before, and during the whole road trip, the two didn't discuss Calvin's comments to Devin. For their meeting today with Brenda, they needed a clear head and decided to table the conversation.

Pulling onto the dirt road, they drove for a mile before reaching a small house, which was connected to a barn. Out walked a big gentleman. Despite the warm June day, he sported cowboy boots and a hat, and was the image of a true Texan.

"Vanessa, come on in here, girl!" said Tommy, beckoning his younger cousin to come towards him for a hug.

Even though there was a big age difference between them, Tommy was one of Vanessa's favorite cousins. He was always exciting to be around, and while they were growing up he was the most fun. After high school he decided to join the military, but when he came back from the war he became a hardcore drug addict. Fed up with what he'd become, one day twenty years ago he made the decision to get help, and had been sober ever since.

"Tommy, meet my fiancé, Devin."

Coming in to shake his hand, Devin felt much gratitude to the man for helping with his mother.

"I can't thank you enough for looking out and helping my mother. I know she can be a lot," he muttered.

"Yes, she can be," Tommy laughed. "But it's been nice having her here."

For a few more minutes Devin and Tommy stood around getting acquainted, while Vanessa swatted mosquitoes. The sound of Vanessa slapping the side of her leg caught the attention of the men.

"Okay, let's go inside before these mosquitoes tear Vanessa up," Tommy chuckled. "Brenda's waiting for us."

With that, he turned around and directed them inside the house. Devin thought he was seeing things when the woman taking dinner out of the oven, with mitts, and who was twenty pounds heavier, turned around, facing him.

"Mom?"

Placing the pan on top of the stove, Brenda grew nervous. She'd messed up, big time, and had caused her family nothing but havoc and pain for years. She was ashamed but knew she had to face her kids and make amends, eventually.

"Hi, Devin," said Brenda, in a timid tone.

Devin didn't move towards her. It had been three months since she arrived in Texas, but his mother looked like a totally different person. What he saw was a brightness in her eyes, a healthy weight and a glow he hadn't seen in her since even before Thaddeus passed away. While Devin looked at his mother in amazement, Vanessa took the opportunity to embrace Brenda.

"Mom, you look great! We're so happy to see you!"

Still at a loss for words, Devin just looked on during the entire dinner as Vanessa asked Brenda questions about her time in Texas. Seeing his mother without a drink in her hand, and in a presentable dress, and cooking, was a new sight, and he couldn't take his eyes off of her. He felt like he was seeing things.

According to Tommy, for the last few months not only had Brenda not been drinking or doing drugs, but she'd been going to church, volunteering at a soup kitchen and attending AA meetings every week. The country seemed to be doing some good for Brenda, who looked healthier and more relaxed, even if a little nervous.

"So, this whole time all we needed to do was get you out of the city?" asked Devin skeptically.

"Devin, a lot of people think they can beat addiction just by moving somewhere but it's deeper than that. An addict has to want to change. Your mom made that decision because she was ready."

Unconvinced, Devin just dabbed the corners of his mouth before taking a sip of lemonade. Dinner came to an end and Brenda jumped up to begin cleaning up and washing the dishes.

"Brenda, don't you want to spend some time with Devin? I got the dishes tonight, go enjoy your son," Tommy suggested.

Brenda looked like a deer in headlights as she thought about the uncomfortable conversations that lay ahead for her and her children. Pasting on a smile, she invited Devin outside for a walk.

Unlike the city, the night sky in Texas was full of stars, and it was beautiful. The pair walked for a few minutes before Brenda stopped at a bench next to a lake.

"Devin, I'm on step nine in the AA big book, and I have some amends to make to you, if that's okay."

"You just need to say you're sorry?"

"Amends aren't really an apology, they're really about acknowledging the things I've done, and figuring out where we go from here."

Thinking about it for a moment, Devin realized he didn't want acknowledgment. He was angry and hurt and unsure of how to express it.

"Come on, let's have a seat."

Taking his hand, she looked at him until he lifted his head and stared into her clear, bright eyes that were no longer the pale yellow or tinted red.

"I've let you and your brother down, time and time again," she began solemnly. "Devin, I made you grow up quicker than you should have. What can I do to fix this?"

Scooting closer to him, she pulled him into her arms, something she hadn't done in decades, and barely did when he was a kid. Tense, his shoulders began to slowly fall as the weight of his mother's addiction and the family drama seemingly melted away. Tears erupted from both mother and son. Looking up, his eyes pleaded with Brenda.

"Mom, please. I just want you to stay how you are now. Healthy and sober. Me and Julian need you. The real you."

Crying in each other's arms, for the first time, Brenda made that promise, and meant it.

CHAPTER 24

FAMILY GET TOGETHER

"I can't believe I let you talk me into going to this thing," said a scowling Devin.

After his argument with Vanessa's father, he was hoping to avoid him for the remainder of the trip, but Taryn had insisted on hosting a crawfish boil for them before they left the next day, and Calvin was sure to be in attendance.

"I know, baby, but maybe my dad won't even show up."

"Nah, he'll be there. He likes to get out the house and spread his negativity. He's not going to pass up this chance."

"I wish your mother could have come, but I know she has to stick to her routine this early in her recovery."

Holding hand's, Devin and Vanessa exited the car and walked to the gate leading to the backyard of Taryn's house. Music was playing and cars lined the street. They were about an hour late, but that was because Devin had refused to get dressed. Thanks to Vanessa's sex appeal, she was able to get him out the door with promises of a great evening. As soon as the gate flew open, Taryn's son, Trey, ran towards Vanessa, almost pushing her down.

"Wow, Trey! You started the party without me?" asked Vanessa, who had separated from Devin and was now being led by her nephew to the backyard. Taryn, who had purchased her home two years prior, had done a great job renovating and decorating. The backyard was spacious and well furnished with a big screen television in the center of it. Family and friends mingled as they enjoyed the crawfish and camaraderie. Even Kevin, Taryn's estranged husband, was there, laughing and serving food alongside his wife. It looked like the two of them were working things out, or at least trying to show a united front for their son, Trey. Devin liked Kevin and hoped the rumors of his infidelity weren't true.

"I'm so glad y'all made it!" said Celeste who had watched them enter from the kitchen window. Wiping her hands on the towel in front of her to get rid of the leftover food she'd been preparing, she smiled.

"I have some snow crabs just for you, I know how much you love them. They're not your Maryland crabs but I think you'll enjoy them," she said, making Devin's day.

While Vanessa went to say hello to her family and play with Trey, Devin followed her mother to the kitchen to get his special meal. Sliding open the screen to the patio, he immediately saw Calvin sitting on the couch and quickly turned around, suddenly uninterested in his crab legs.

"I'll eat later, thank you."

Seeing Devin trying to avoid him, Calvin stood from the couch and walked towards him.

"Devin, I'd like to talk to you if that's okay."

Out of respect for Vanessa, Devin stopped and turned

towards the older man.

"Let me grab us some beers and we can find somewhere to sit and talk for a bit," Calvin continued.

Remaining quiet, afraid of what he might say, Devin followed his lead. Finally, beers in hand, the two men were seated in the family room, away from the crowd and noise.

"When my wife calls me out on something, I listen," he began. "I talk a lot and usually she lets me, but this time I went too far. She never gets mad and that woman is mad as hell at me right now. She hasn't talked to me since the other day when y'all left the house."

Devin sat silently and listened on.

"Anyway, I've been doing some thinking the last couple of days and I owe you an apology. What I said about your mom was completely out of line."

Devin slammed the beer onto the table and leaned forward.

"What about the snide remarks about my sexuality or that car accident comment you made? You sorry for those too?"

Calvin looked like he wanted to lash out at Devin, but a quick glance towards Celeste, who was sneaking peeks toward them, made him stop. Taking a minute to gather his thoughts, he decided for the first time with someone other than Celeste, to be vulnerable.

"Devin, since I met my wife I've always felt a little undeserving. Here comes this woman from a prestigious family, with her father being Isaiah Barrett, and she's actually interested in little ole me from a little country town in East Texas. Our relationship started off with me feeling inferior, and not good enough for her. Even though I knew

Celeste and my girls loved and respected me, I always felt like I was lacking. This might sound selfish, but once Bishop Barrett passed away, I thought maybe my wife and daughters would lean on me more. Instead, you showed up with your pedigree, accomplishments, and I once again felt less than. Without realizing it I lashed out at you, and that's on me. I'm sorry for that because I haven't been fair. Truth be told, I think you're a solid guy, and I apologize for the comments about your sexuality, and definitely for bringing your mother into this. I was wrong."

The solemn look on Calvin's face told Devin that he really did regret how he'd been acting, and that was all he needed to hear.

"Sir, my father's name is mostly associated with crooked deals and murder. Now, I still don't know the truth about what all he did or did not do, but I think Vanessa is very blessed to have you. She knows how much you adore her and she has so much love for you. Whenever something breaks around the house, or I forget something at the store, she always says, my daddy would know how to do this, my daddy would have done that. It's sweet but annoying," laughed Devin. "No one can replace you, it's not even possible."

Smiling from ear to ear, Calvin didn't know his baby-girl talked about him like that.

"You know what? This wasn't so bad. Maybe I should apologize to Kevin next for what happened at Pappadeaux last year."

"Sir, with all due respect, after that ass whooping he gave you in the restaurant I think you should just leave that situation alone," laughed Devin. Surprisingly, Calvin joined in the laughter and the two men talked more over crabs, crawfish and beer, and enjoyed each other's company for the first time.

CHAPTER 25

BACK AT HOME

The trip down to Houston proved to be successful. On the three-hour flight back home, Devin used the time to catch up on the news. For most of the trip, he had unplugged, wanting to be in the moment, and was happy that he did. Scrolling through articles online, he smiled when he came across a photo of him with his mother. Leave it to Darlene to make sure important moments were captured. Devin couldn't wait to tell Julian all about their mom's progress.

Leaning over to kiss Vanessa's forehead as she slept soundly on his shoulder, he was grateful to her for initiating this intervention and retreat for his mother.

A few hours later they sat in bumper-to-bumper traffic on Interstate 95, as their Uber driver impatiently sounded the horn to his Tesla, willing the driver in front of him to speed up, even though there was nowhere for any of them to go. The ride home was triggering for Devin, thanks to his recent car accident, so to keep his mind occupied he decided to spend the time in the car returning some calls.

First on the callback list was his brother, but before he could dial Julian's number, his phone lit up. It was Regis.

"Hey, we just landed in Baltimore, and are headed home."

"Great, how was Houston? Brenda okay?"

"She's great, I'll tell you more about that later."

"Good to hear! I also heard the wonderful news about that mother and son from the car accident. They're on the mend. It's a good thing that little situation worked itself out, isn't it?" chuckled Regis.

"What do you mean?" asked Devin, wondering what he was talking about.

"Oh, come on, Devin, if those two had died it would've been a shit storm. Your campaign probably wouldn't have survived a tragedy like that. For a second, I thought I was going to have to handle it, if you know what I mean, but I'm glad it didn't come to that. You'll probably still have to pay them some hush money. People like that are always looking for a quick payday. My guess is they're already looking for a lawyer."

Annoyed with what he was hearing, Devin's response made Vanessa lean in to hear more.

"I know what you're capable of, but to be clear, that's not what I'm about, so don't even joke about doing something unethical on my behalf."

"Wow, alright! You're so much like your old man but sometimes I forget. You want the power and prestige but not everything that comes with it. Newsflash Devin, sometimes you have to get your hands a little dirty. I admire you for trying to stay above the fray, but this is politics, eat or get eaten. It's that simple."

Vanessa looked from the phone to Devin and cut her eyes. Regis continued.

"In other news, I have some more donors for you to consider. Check your email for the list when you can."

Regis was hoping to end the call on a high note with that bit of news, but Devin was too irritated.

"Great, thanks. Call you later in the week," said Devin before quickly hanging up.

"I know you want to win but that man is the Devil," mumbled Vanessa, next to him.

"He's not always so cutthroat," said Devin, trying to take up for Regis. But even as he said this, the comment about handling the situation with the mother and the kid from the accident, left him unsure.

"Mmhm," snorted Vanessa, unconvinced.

To take his mind off of Regis, Devin made a call to Darlene, who was happy to hear they were back home and on track to return to the campaign trail. According to her, poll numbers after the visit with his mother were excellent, and the media was backing off. Devin was relieved at this news. Promising to review an email, the two hung up, and Devin dialed his brother. Answering on the first ring, Devin jumped into conversation.

"You finally back in Maryland or you still in Cali with Avery?"

"I'm back, man, and listen to this shit. You won't believe it—"

Always one for the dramatics, he paused until Devin asked, "Okay Julian, won't believe what?"

"Avery's pregnant!" yelled Julian so loud that Vanessa, who was close enough to hear the news despite the call not being on speaker, sat up straight.

"Congratulations!" she exclaimed and jumped up and down in her seat as if Julian could see her excitement.

Stunned, Devin was amazed at how happy Julian sounded. Who knew his playboy little brother even wanted children? He'd never once heard him talk about wanting a family of his own. Devin was having a difficult time imagining him as a father, and was interested to see how he would handle fatherhood.

"You better do right by my girl, Avery," Vanessa said.

"I'm working on that, Sis. Hey, Devin, meet me for some drinks this week, we have to catch up on everything that's been happening."

"Bet, we clearly have a lot to chat about, just let me know when and where."

CHAPTER 26

BURDEN OF PROOF

Head scarf on firm and tight, Vanessa fixed her glasses and repositioned her laptop to make her makeshift work area on the couch more comfortable. She had files spread out in front of her on the coffee table. They held documents that had been sent to her by a friend in the FBI. Vanessa was uninterested in hearing about all the things she already knew about Regis Adams, all outlined in his recent feature story in *Impact.* The article talked about how he'd picked himself up by his bootstraps, worked hard and caught the attention of the former Governor of Maryland.

No, Vanessa wanted to know the things people only whispered about, like the tales of his corrupt practices, unethical agendas and blackmail. To get to the bottom of it all she'd requested to see every piece of paper that could possibly include any information on his shady moves. She didn't understand how he'd been in Devin's life all of these years and he had never taken the time to really look into all the stories surrounding Regis.

That ends today, she thought to herself. Reaching for the files, she sat back Indian style and started skimming each one. They were in chronological order, from his early years to his most recent business ventures. Selecting the one marked childhood, she went to work. Totally engrossed in what she was finding out, for two hours Vanessa chewed on her pen, stunned at all the information she was learning. The documents did not explicitly outline Regis's wrongdoings, but he was mentioned alongside some of the biggest scandals in politics or businesses, spanning decades, beginning with his time with Governor Nichols in 1973.

To help visualize the information in the papers she was reading, Vanessa grabbed a loose-leaf notebook and drew a timeline on a page. On it she included the names of politicians and capitalists that Regis had worked with over the years. Then, she googled each name to see where they were currently. Out of a list of twelve, only five seemed completely legit. The others had been involved in crimes and schemes of diverse types.

Three politicians were in jail for accepting bribes. Cryptocurrency investor Frank Lispy had filed bankruptcy, Congressman Henderson had resigned following a sex scandal, Congressman Rucker had been linked to a bribery ring before being murdered, and of course there was Devin's father, Thaddeus, accused of corruption and eventually murder. Lifting her pen from the timeline, Vanessa scrunched up her face. For so long, Congressman Rucker had only been tied to Thaddeus, but it was Regis who introduced the two, and he'd had a working relationship with the Congressman well before Thaddeus did. As strange as this seemed to Vanessa, her mind blew when she got to the donor folder.

She wanted to know all the people Regis had secured for Devin, and her research into them left her speechless.

Reaching for her phone, she dialed Devin's number. He answered on the second ring and could hear the anxiety in his fiancée's voice when she said, *"Get home, now."*

CHAPTER 27

THE APPROACH

Charles Welsh played with the flimsy paper, wondering if it would be a good idea to use it. Embossed on the back of the card was Supervisory Special Agent, Sandra Perry's cell phone number. The night before, as he sifted through old files, a four-by-six surveillance photo fell from one of the folders. It showed a smiling Sandra sitting next to Thaddeus at a hotel bar. It reminded Welsh that Sandra had initially worked with Thaddeus. Figuring she would be the only person willing and able to help him reopen the investigation, he contemplated reaching out. Finally, he picked up his phone and dialed the numbers before placing the call on speaker.

"Sandra," came the soft yet authoritative voice he recalled from their elevator meeting.

"Ma'am, sorry to bother you, this is Charles Welsh, we recently reconnected."

"Yes, of course, how are you? What can I do for you?"

"Well, there's a case I'm interested in reopening. I

wanted to see if I could get a moment of your time before the end of the week to discuss it."

"A meeting request should go through the proper channels," she said before pausing.

"But I'd like to hear what you've come across. My lunch plans for tomorrow were just cancelled, how about we meet at around one and I have my assistant send you the details?"

"Thank you, I'll be there."

The small section sat secluded and towards the back of the restaurant, away from the crowd of patrons on their lunch breaks. Welsh had just finished telling Sandra all about his desire to reopen the Thaddeus Simmons case, and all he had learned from Ian, which included the new information from Jacob. Sandra remained quiet as she used her fork to pick through her salad.

"Last time I worked on this case it didn't turn out so great for me," she said.

"I know ma'am but this time we have some solid leads. The evidence alone from Jacob, his old friend and business partner, helps us greatly."

Placing her fork down and pushing her bowl away, the high-ranking federal official looked Welsh square in the eyes.

"We've had an interest in Regis Adams for years. When Thaddeus entered the picture and started getting cozy with him we decided to make him our inside man. We used his weakness for women to our advantage. Luckily for us his secretary Tara had a rap sheet a mile long, so it wasn't hard to get her on board as an informant. She obtained information for us on Thaddeus, and evidence of some of his illegal activities, and we used that material against him. Cornering him outside of a coffee shop, I gave him my business card and told him it was in his best interest to call me. He called, we met up and he agreed to turn on Regis if he received immunity. He did, and his family and finances were protected."

Welsh waited for her to say more but she just took a second to take a sip of her water and looked off in the distance with a blank stare. Finally, she continued. After securing Thaddeus as a criminal informant, Sandra began speaking with him weekly. Together, over the course of several months, they were able to build a solid case against Regis. In the beginning, Thaddeus tried sleeping with Sandra, but she was able to establish boundaries early on with him, earning his respect. Some would even say they had become friends. This was why when the bureau found out that it was she who alerted Thaddeus about the raid that morning, they blamed her for his attempted escape and accused her of obstruction of justice. Sandra would never forget that day.

Dialing Thaddeus's number, her heart pounded. Sandra had tried calling her informant four times, and each time got his voicemail. Gnawing at her fingernail, a nervous habit she'd developed as a child, she wondered what to do next. News had come to her just a few minutes earlier that Congressman Paul Rucker had been shot and killed. Based on the word of the only witness, a working girl whom the

FBI later tracked down, the feds believed the murder was the work of businessman Thaddeus Simmons, her criminal informant. Sandra didn't believe for a second that Thaddeus was responsible for the hit, and couldn't understand why the bureau was acting so quickly on the word of the woman who ran away from the scene of the crime.

Thaddeus had a good deal in place with the FBI, there was no way he would ruin that. It didn't make sense to her, so against her better judgment, she called his office to warn him that her colleagues were coming to raid his office. Minutes went by before her phone rang.

"Hey, Sandra, sorry I missed your calls. Regis is here, and he's acting kind of strange…"

"Thaddeus, get out of there now."

"What are you talking about?"

"Paul Rucker was found dead, they think you did it."

"What?" he gasped.

Sandra had spoken briefly with Thaddeus following his meeting with Paul Rucker and Regis, and was aware that Paul was freaking out about a reporter reaching out to him.

"It has to be Regis, Sandra! He freaked out when he thought Rucker was going to go public with the bribes and corruption schemes."

Sandra agreed, but before they could make a plan, one of Thaddeus's security guards interrupted their talk. Agents of the FBI had arrived, and in their search for Thaddeus, they were causing an uproar on the main floor.

"Go to your plane, and get to your attorney's office right now. I'll figure this out."

Unfortunately, Thaddeus never made it off the building in his helicopter. In the days that followed, Sandra tried to plead his case, but everyone believed she was compromised and had gotten too close to Thaddeus. Some suspected she'd slept with the businessman, further destroying her reputation.

"It took me ten years to rebuild my reputation and I can't afford to let the case that almost ruined my career all those years ago return and completely destroy all of my hard work. With that said, let's work on this quietly for now. What Jacob shared so far sounds hopeful, but who we really need to talk to is Brittany Garcia. I know where you can find her."

Welsh grimaced at the mention of the woman he'd been trying to track down and question all those years ago. Chasing behind her caused him to be chased down himself, and put in a wheelchair for the rest of his life. Snapping out of the depressing memory, Welsh realized what she'd just said.

"Wait, you know where Brittany is?"

"Yes, and you might know too. Ever heard of Tattoo Inc.?"

Staring blankly at Sandra, Welsh couldn't understand what a tattoo parlor had to do with the only witness from the case. Noticing his confusion, she pulled out her phone, pressed some buttons and slid it across the table for Welsh to see. On the screen was an Instagram account showing a group of women posing for a reality show premiere. The woman on the far left looked familiar but not quite like the girl from several years before.

"The one in the red, that's her. After the murder, she

split town for a couple of years, then suddenly resurfaced, and with a lot more money. Most people don't know this, because it wasn't made public, but Brittany wasn't even at the age of consent when she was with Paul. She was just a kid. I've always thought that Regis somehow got to her and convinced her to lie in her testimony in exchange for some money. When she came back to Maryland from wherever she had gone, she got custody of her younger brother, who was in foster care, enrolled in college where she earned a bachelor's degree in business, then opened a tattoo shop."

It was true, Brittany Garcia had done a full three-sixty since her days of selling her body and doing drugs. The night that Congressman Paul Rucker was killed in front of her changed her life drastically, and now with six tattoo parlors across the U.S. and one is London, she was skilled and hugely successful.

"I knew something was up so I decided to keep up with her all of these years. She's in her early thirties now and running one of the most popular tattoo shops in the world. People come from all over to see her, and she's done work for celebrities. She's kind of like a celebrity now herself."

"Well, what would be our way in with her? It's been a long time, and it seems like she's been living a good life. What reason would she have to turn Regis in after he did all of that for her?"

"Her two weaknesses are her younger brother and her boyfriend. We need to do a deep dive into both of them and find our area of opportunity."

"Sounds good to me, I'll start looking into their records right away."

Good-byes were exchanged and as Welsh crossed the

street to head back to the office, he sent a quick text to Ian.

Welsh: The case is reopened.

Ian: It's on.

For the first time since he could remember, Welsh smiled. He finally felt like the world was on his side and he couldn't wait to see what would happen next.

CHAPTER 28

HAPPY HOUR

Clinking their glasses, Devin and Julian toasted to a guy's night out. Taking a sip of his drink, Devin flagged the bartender over.

"Can we get a shot of whiskey too? My kid brother just found out he's having a kid."

Familiar with the brothers, the bartender even took a shot with them and collected the glasses.

"So how is Avery doing? When's the baby due?"

Leaning against the bar with a massive smile, Julian opened his wallet and produced a sonogram.

"She's doing good, man. Still having some morning sickness but we're out of the first trimester now so the doctor said the nausea should subside, but we'll see."

"Oh, we?" joked Devin, surveying the image. "Man, I can't even lie, you haven't looked this happy in years and it's nice to see. It's like you're a changed man, already."

Playfully shoving him, Julian smiled.

"I want her to move out here, but she keeps turning

down the idea."

"Jules, you have to give her some more time. A lot is happening fast, give her a chance to digest it all."

Julian knew he was right, but refused to give up on the idea. The thought of waking up to Avery and their baby every day and to be part of a real family made him want to push to make that dream come true. Refocusing his attention, he gave his older brother a once-over.

"I'm really happy you're okay after that accident. You had us worried, D."

"I appreciate it, I'm just glad everyone made it out of the crash alive."

"What was up with the car?"

"I still have to follow up with Uncle Jacob to see what he found out about my brakes. It's strange, especially since I've never had issues with that car. I wish it never happened, but the accident did allow me to re-connect with Mom."

"So, she looks good in person? We FaceTime every week, and I can tell she's gained her weight back."

"She's beautiful, man! Skin glowing, healthy weight, her hair is all braided up and she just looks free. Like she's no longer burdened by life. Her eyes are clear and bright, it's like there's new life in them. I have to give it to you and Vanessa, y'all made the right call getting her to Houston."

"To be fair, Mom asked us for help. She was tired, finally at her bottom."

The two took a moment to sink into their thoughts. The trauma of having grown up with an alcoholic was never lost on them.

"Well, we have two good things to report, but I found out some shit yesterday that blew my mind."

Crossing his arms, Julian could tell by the anger in his brother's voice, that this next set of news wasn't good.

"Regis has been on some creep shit lately. Apparently, Vanessa heard him talking to Uncle Jacob at your party, and he said some weird stuff, even about Dad. Afterwards Vanessa thought it would be a good idea to look into Regis's affairs. I can't believe I didn't do that before I let him become so involved with my campaign."

"Nah bro, don't start that. You let him become involved because we've always trusted him. Dad trusted him so it's natural that we did too. He's been nothing but good to us over the years."

Neither brother said this out loud, but they each felt dumb for trusting anyone their father had trusted. At the end of the day, Regis was supposed to go to jail for various crimes, and no one knew who he had been working with. Julian wasn't liking where the conversation was going, and slowly sipped on his beer as his brother finished sharing what he'd just learned from Vanessa.

Dropping everything at the campaign headquarters to drive home and check on Vanessa, Devin was surprised at what he came home to. Laptop open, files scattered around the coffee table and on the floor of the living room, Devin walked into chaos and toward a very angry Vanessa.

"That muthafucka ain't shit, Devin. I knew something was up with him."

"Baby, calm down and tell me what's going on."

"I looked into Regis and into all the people he's been bringing onto and around your campaign."

Devin watched Vanessa as she stood up from the couch and carried a stack of papers over to the dining room table for him to see.

"These donors are connected to businesses and people you would never support or ever consider taking money from, Devin. Regis is setting you up. He knows you trust him, so he's banking on you never researching these donors for yourself, but I'm so glad that I did. I don't know his angle, but from what I can tell he's setting you up somehow."

Devin remained quiet while he reviewed the list of donors and Vanessa's notes next to their names. On the surface they seemed like legit donors, but Vanessa's thorough review proved that there was more to them.

Names of executives from two of the largest prison companies were on the list. It was a well-known fact that Devin was against for-profit prisons, and he was sure Regis was well aware of this. Cursing under his breath he read on. The list included names of pro-gun supporters and drug companies, but what really stood out to Devin were the names that didn't include a summary next to them. This meant Vanessa couldn't get any information on them, making them more dangerous than the others. Shaking his head at the thought of who those people could be, he closed his eyes and went through a series of emotions: shock, denial, sadness, and most of all, anger.

"One other thing, babe."

Pulling out a separate pile of folders, Vanessa had copies of fallen politicians and businessmen, including his father and Congressman Rucker.

"What does my dad have to do with any of this?"

"All of these people have one thing in common. They

have some type of connection to Regis."

Julian sat stunned. Regis had been in their lives since they were kids. He'd attended graduations, birthdays, and had connected them with some of the most important and powerful people in the world. What was his angle?

"Oh, he's a snake," was all Julian could get out.

"Apparently Regis is the one who introduced Paul Rucker to Dad. There's something going on here, and we need to figure this out."

"I agree. Call Uncle Jacob, if anybody knows anything about this, it'll be him."

"You're right, but the real question is, if Uncle Jacob knew about all this, why didn't he do something about it from jump, or at least say something when Regis joined my team?"

Julian shook his head in agreement. Standing up from their barstools, the brothers prepared to leave, with a lot on their minds. For the first time, Julian had thoughts apart from Avery and the baby, and they were unsettling.

Sitting across the street, Jade watched as Julian dapped up his brother and got in his waiting car. Julian had been dodging her for weeks, since around the time of his birthday party, and she had had enough. Watching him drive off, she ducked down low to avoid being spotted. Happy that he hadn't been out to meet some girl, Jade started her car and headed home, thinking about her first date with Julian.

Walking into the city's best rooftop lounge, which

provided a perfect panoramic view of Baltimore, Jade gasped. Clearly captivated by the charm of the city and the presence of fine dining mixed with beautiful people who smelled of money, the young girl from the projects had never seen anything like it. At that moment, Jade knew she had made it, or was at least headed in that direction.

Seated at a small table closest to the edge where the view began, Julian admired his date's large chest, which matched well with her round ass. *I'm gonna have fun with this one*, he thought, as he licked his lips in anticipation of what was to come after drinks and dessert. The pair had had dinner downstairs earlier, and afterwards decided to venture upstairs.

With his hand on her leg under the table, he slowly shifted his hands lower until he palmed her inner thigh. Shifting in her seat and pushing her chair closer, it was clear she wanted more.

Familiar with the staff, Julian paused from feeling her up and motioned for a staff member to come over. Not even a minute later, the two were led behind a rope, which placed them on the other side of the terrace. The area was more isolated and private, but there were still a few people milling around nearby. Lowering his frame to wrap her in his arms, he planted small kisses on her until she lifted her face to meet his lips, then he began devouring her mouth in his. Slowly, Julian lowered his hands to grip her ass. After feeling for underwear, he found none. Noticing his hands exploring, she grinned up at him and said, "I don't have anything on."

Oh, it's about to go down, he thought to himself. Taking her by the hand he led her to the exit leading to the stairway.

Within seconds of the door shutting, Jade had her dress hiked up, encouraging Julian to take her however he wanted to. Leading her to the stairs, he unbuckled his belt before sliding out of his high-priced tailored slacks. Leaning down to meet her body, he knelt beside the stair and decided to taste Jade. Sliding his tongue in and out of her juices, he lingered at her clit and softly began running his tongue over it. When he was done, she shifted to return the favor.

Bringing her down to the floor, Julian said, "This is about you."

For a few seconds he kissed her body before wrapping her legs around himself and entering her while she squealed in pleasure. Right there, on the rooftop bar in the stairway, Jade knew she'd found her forever person.

CHAPTER 29

THE STRATEGY

Regis sat awake in bed on Sunday morning with a lot on his mind. Born in Baltimore, he had the typical rags to riches hood story. Raised by a single mother of three in a rough part of town, his mother worked three jobs and was never home with him or his two sisters. Believing he was the man of the house, and that he needed to help his mother, fourteen-year-old Regis joined a crew in West Baltimore and became a corner boy. He quickly rose up in rank when the street leaders realized he had potential. Regis did what he was told, kept his head down, wasn't careless with the product and was always right with the money.

Midnight, a street captain who was both respected and feared in the game, took a liking to Regis. He began giving him more responsibilities, and on his sixteenth birthday Midnight promoted him to lieutenant. Regis wasn't sure if he wanted it, but didn't dare tell Midnight 'no.'

Unlike his friends, Regis was still enrolled in high school, a magnet school for gifted kids, and he did well enough in his classes to pass each quarter. He wanted more than what the street life could offer him, but wasn't sure what he wanted or how to get there. On a field trip to the Governor's mansion with his American Politics class one day, his future was all Regis could think about.

With thoughts of his promotion to lieutenant clouding his mind, he didn't realize the school bus had parked in front of the federal building in Annapolis until kids stood up from their seats to file off. This trip was no doubt a way for the governor and his people to check low-income communities off their list. A tour guide showed them around the mansion, and then, somewhere during the middle of the visit, there was a commotion.

Secret service led Gregory Nichols, the 56th Governor of Maryland, towards the small group of students.

"I heard we had some visitors, I had to come and see for myself," said Governor Nichols, smiling.

Introductions were made before Governor Nichols shared a few words with the group, providing details about his job and the importance of politics in the world. He spoke like he was talking to a room full of idiots, and Regis was bored. Noticing the young man in the back who seemed uninterested and ready to go, Governor Nichols called over to him.

"You in the back, what's your name?"

Surprised he was getting called on and trying to look cool, Regis gave a half shrug, stood up a little straighter and announced his name with authority, like he was the King of Zamunda.

"Well, Regis, you look like you're about to go to sleep standing up. Am I boring you?"

The teacher tried to jump in and apologize but Governor Nichols held his hand up and waited for Regis to respond.

"Governor, this is a waste of time. You're talking about the branches of government like we're in elementary school. I don't know if you know this but we go to a magnet school, we're black not dumb, sir."

Playing on the brief pause, Regis continued.

"What I am interested in is where you stand on the Fair Housing Act. You skirt around that question every time you're asked about it on television. You did the same thing a few years ago with the Civil Rights Act."

Mouth gaped open, Governor Nichols was at a loss for words. A prominent politician for decades, he was highly respected and not used to being challenged, especially by children or in public.

"Regis, I appreciate your question," said the Governor, gathering his thoughts. "I assure you I support that act and have been working with representatives to get that legislation passed."

Nichols remained for another five minutes before jetting off to a meeting. The class finished for the day. When returning to the bus, Regis was handed a business card by security. On the back of the card, in bold hand-written lettering it said 'Call Me' with an unfamiliar number underneath the instructions. Intrigued, Regis pocketed the card and jumped on the bus. That day changed Regis's life forever. Instead of taking the promotion that would have undoubtedly gotten him locked up or killed, he took the opportunity that seemed like a safer and more rewarding bet. Governor Nichols took Regis out of the streets and placed him in a boardroom.

Regis became the governor's star pupil. Nichols taught him everything he knew about business and politics—the good and the bad. When it was time for college, Nichols paid for him to go to one of the most impressive schools. After serving two terms, the former Governor moved to Connecticut with his wife, leaving the business of politics to Regis, but while he disappeared behind the scenes, Nichols was still, in fact, very present and pulling strings that many were not aware of.

"Honey, are you okay?" interrupted Regis's wife, Charlotte.

It was 7 a.m. and she was up, getting dressed for church. Regis never missed church, it was part of his façade and a great opportunity for him to rub elbows with prestigious men and women, but today he wasn't feeling it. Facing her husband, Charlotte put her earrings on as she did a full body scan of him. She could tell he'd been up all night, and was concerned. His crinkled brows told her he had a lot on his mind.

"That call you were on before we went to bed kept you up, didn't it?"

Regis let out a grunting sound that told her not to push.

"Well, I'm leaving for church soon, are you coming today?"

Silence followed. Grabbing her purse, Charlotte took one final look at Regis, then turned to leave. They'd known each other since they were kids and had been married for many years. She knew Regis like the back of her hand.

Whatever was worrying him, she knew it would all be okay. Her husband always did what needed to be done and worked things out. His sharp mind and strategic thinking were what she loved the most about him.

Hearing the door close downstairs, Regis slowly sat up, slid into his house shoes and threw on his R.A. monogrammed robe. Shuffling to the kitchen, he made a cup of coffee and leaned against the counter in deep thought. Before lying down the night before, he had received a call from a source of his who alerted him whenever something was awry. Whenever there were whispers about anything concerning him, he contacted Regis.

In this case, the source reached out to inform Regis that he was back under investigation. Not only had the FBI reopened Thaddeus and Congressman Paul Rucker's murder cases, but a nosey journalist had been calling around, asking questions. To top things off, Regis learned that Vanessa had requested files on him and the donor list he'd created for Devin's campaign. Usually calm under pressure, Regis uncharacteristically found himself tensing up, thinking about Thaddeus Simmons.

Thaddeus had been the closest thing he'd had to a protégé, even though they were close in age at nine years apart, and he was one of the few people Regis trusted. The two met at the Pentagon at an event for fallen soldiers, shortly after Thaddeus founded Simmons Enterprises, and had hit it off. Regis was instrumental in Thaddeus's success, introducing him to the people he needed to know to make his business lucrative. Somewhere along the journey, Thaddeus, who started off as an honest businessman, became hungry for power and so enamored with Regis that he heeded most of his advice. The counsel led him to participate in deals and talks that had the potential to lead him down a dark road, which is exactly what happened when he was connected to Paul Rucker.

Grabbing his mug, Regis went to his study and sat at his chess board to play a game. Playing against himself sometimes helped him think. Making the first move, his mind raced back to two decades ago, when he'd received a phone call from his late friend and protégé.

"Hey Regis, it's me. I don't want to say too much over the phone, but Paul just called and he was talking crazy. You both should meet me at my place tonight."

A few hours later, Thaddeus, waiting for his guests to arrive, popped his head into the master bedroom to check on his wife, who as expected, was in a drunk induced sleep and probably wouldn't wake until the morning. After making sure Devin and Julian were also sound asleep in their rooms, he heard the doorbell sound, signaling the arrival of his company. Gently closing the door to the last bedroom, he headed downstairs to greet his visitors. Before the door was fully open, Regis pushed through the frame and walked straight towards Thaddeus's home office.

"What seems to be the problem?" he asked, shooting past him.

"Just go and take a seat, Regis. Paul just pulled up."

"This shit better be important," Regis muttered. "Charlotte made her famous lasagna tonight and I'm hungry, so we're gonna have to hurry this little meeting along."

Behind Regis came Congressman Paul Rucker of

New Jersey. Barely looking Thaddeus in the eye as he approached, it was obvious that he had something on his mind. Noticing his discomfort, Thaddeus said nothing as he shut the door and led him to the back. Seated and quiet, Regis was getting annoyed with the Congressman.

"What are we doing here, Paul? Speak up for Christ sake."

Paul Rucker was in his early forties and known for picking up prostitutes, dabbling in drugs and taking bribes, but he wasn't always like that. At one time he was one of the good guys, one in whom people could put their trust. He was a Jewish kid from New Jersey, and even though he didn't come from a lot of money, his family worked hard, providing him many opportunities. That, along with his book smarts, afforded him a successful career in politics. He was relatable and funny, but a few years after joining the House of Representatives, things went downhill. Some would say this was after he met the infamous Regis Adams.

Regis had a way of spotting the broken bird in the bunch and that's exactly what happened the day he met a young Paul Rucker. One could tell that Paul was starving for power, money and a life he'd always envisioned. Regis saw all of this in his eyes the first time they talked and decided to zero in on him. Regis's ability to make people feel safe was superb. He was a master manipulator and practiced his skills every chance he got. His approach was crafty and he always appeared genuine. He lured people in, mostly younger politicians, with introductions and invites to special functions with the nation's most wealthy and powerful people, then he would work to establish lucrative relationships with the elite. He was somewhat of a crooked lobbyist. Business leaders leaned on him for his political connections, and politicians liked the extra cash they knew he would eventually send their way. The few and influential knew that Regis was the man to go to if you needed things done, and while they suspected him of resorting to certain unethical methods like blackmail or coercion, they turned a blind eye to his methods and kept their mouths shut. Rumor had it there was someone even more powerful than Regis pulling the strings from behind the scenes.

Within months of meeting Regis, Paul had accepted bribes from defense contractors in exchange for steering government contracts their way, which was how Paul met Thaddeus. Regis didn't foresee Paul going off the deep end but that's exactly what he did. The more money and gifts the young Congressman received the worse his behavior became. He picked up prostitutes in his luxury two-seater convertible Benz, got drunk and jumped off the side of his new yacht in Barbados, bought two new homes, and much more. Since walking in on him snorting cocaine in their bathroom a couple of weeks earlier, his wife had been threatening to take their kids and leave if he didn't straighten out, but Paul didn't believe her.

"I had a journalist call me at home this morning." Paul started. "I was taking a sip from my first cup of jo for the day, and Ian Thompson, that big time reporter came right out and asked if I've been taking bribes. Damn near spit out my coffee all over the newspaper!"

"Well what did you tell him?"

"I told him I didn't appreciate being harassed at home and that I had no comment, then hung up. He called back and left a voicemail. Here, listen."

Flipping open his phone, he placed the message on speaker.

"Sir, this is Ian Thompson with the *The Daily Sun*. Please call me back before midnight, or this story will be published in time for the morning paper. I would like to hear what you have to say, I'm sure it's more than 'no comment,' but something will be printed tomorrow, regardless."

Paul ended the message and looked hurriedly between Regis and Thaddeus.

"What am I supposed to do? Midnight is in a few hours, should I just come clean?"

"No!" said Regis and Thaddeus in unison.

"Boy, why are you so damn soft," growled Regis. "Saying anything will place us and a lot of other people in an unnecessary predicament!"

"Okay! Then what do I do?" he asked, fidgeting. It was obvious he was high off of something, making the situation worse.

"I'll handle it, just go home and sleep off whatever you're on."

Whenever Regis said he would handle something, everyone knew not to ask any questions. After their meeting, Regis and Paul walked to their cars. Before driving off the property, Regis looked down and realized he'd left his phone in Thaddeus's office. Jumping out, he jogged to the door and let himself in. Walking towards the study, he overheard Thaddeus on the phone with what sounded like a woman.

"Sandra, I'll get you what you need. I'm telling you, as long as me and my family are protected you can count on me."

Shocked into place, Regis couldn't move. Sandra was

the name of a federal agent who'd been investigating him for almost a year. What was he doing on the phone with her? Could she really have gotten Thaddeus, his friend, on her side?

Retreating outside, Regis sat in his car for a minute before deciding to go back and knock on the front door, like he had not just been inside and present for Thaddeus's private phone call. Coming to the door, Thaddeus smiled and acted as if everything was normal, putting Regis even more on edge. Regardless of the reason, Regis now knew he had two problems to get rid of. A quick call to someone he considered an insider for information confirmed what he'd feared. Thaddeus was working with the feds.

They must have something on him to make him turn on me, Regis said to himself. Whatever the reason, Regis hated people who were disloyal, especially when he'd been good to them.

That same evening, Congressman Rucker was found dead beside his car in the wee hours of the morning. His pants were down to his ankles and it was clear there had been another person present. The perfume in the air made authorities conclude that the other occupant was a woman, probably a prostitute since they were in an area of town known for heavy solicitation. That same day, federal agents located the woman. Caught on a camera from a nearby corner store, Brittany Garcia was seen running from the direction of Paul Rucker's parked car, headed to a local bus stop. Her disheveled hair and tear-stained face with streaks of mascara on her cheeks made everyone clamor to hear her side of the story.

The young woman appeared to be under eighteen but

at the moment, officers only cared about learning who was responsible for killing New Jersey Congressman, Paul Rucker. At first Brittany was overwhelmed by the attention she was receiving, and remained quiet. It wasn't until someone suggested she was behind the murder, that she spoke up. According to Brittany, not only did a man shoot Rucker at close range, but he wore all black with a black ski mask, so she could only make out his eyes. The part of her story that made everyone raise their eyebrows was when she replayed the moments just before the shooting.

"When he raised his gun to shoot Paul, the man said, 'This is for Thaddeus.' Then boom! Dude shot him."

After sharing her story, Brittany sat down with a sketch artist. That same day agents raided Simmons Enterprises, looking for Thaddeus Simmons, whom they believed was behind the assassination of Congressman Rucker. It didn't matter to them that Thaddeus had been working with Agent Sandra Perry of the FBI to take down a corrupt businessman in exchange for immunity. All they cared about was the fact that Thaddeus was named by their only witness. They assumed Thaddeus did it because Paul was planning to share sensitive information that would incriminate him. Information that Sandra wasn't even privy to. Documents highlighting his mis-dealings with Congressman Rucker sealed Thaddeus's fate and he was promptly arrested and faced prison time. A couple of weeks before his trial, Thaddeus Simmons was found hanging in his jail cell.

Finishing up his game of chess, Regis kept his focus on taking down the queen. Just when he found a way to take her, a thought came to him. He needed to see Vanessa. She was digging into his past and that would affect his relationship with Devin and his business. In this case, Vanessa was the queen, and he needed to find out what she knew before putting together a solid plan that would get everyone off his trail, once and for all.

CHAPTER 30

THE WITNESS

It was afternoon when Sandra and Welsh pulled up to a jet-black building that had a sign on its front that read: Tattoo Inc., in big, white block letters. She could have assigned an agent to accompany Welsh on this visit, but figured her knowledge of the former witness and the case would be advantageous in obtaining the right information.

Putting the SUV in park, she was preparing to get out to retrieve Welsh's wheelchair from the trunk, when a huge commotion took place on the steps of the building. A couple had just appeared from inside, and their voices were raised to a tone that invited anyone nearby into their argument. A small man ran after them with a gigantic camera, hoping to capture the intensity that was happening for viewers. The front door opened once more and out came a curvy woman who displayed vibrant art on almost every part of her body, except her face. She was beautiful, and at that moment she was livid.

"I'm not with this shit, y'all!"

The popular tattoo artist had spent the last four hours tattooing Ghost, an Atlanta based Grammy nominated rapper, when his girlfriend Pumpkin showed up with a camera crew from their reality show *Toxic in Love* and caused a disturbance. The couple was known for their antics, their crazy relationship and for the stunts Pumpkin would pull, like getting his name tatted on her in six places and buying a gold tooth with his photo in it. Having entertainers and celebrities come for her work was always great publicity for her business, but Brittany didn't like drama and confusion, especially in her place of business. Hands on her hips, Brittany watched Pumpkin run and jump on Ghost's back. Swatting her off like a fly, he let her fall to the pavement and cry out for help. Security appeared and eventually the situation was under control. Shaking her head, Brittany turned to go back inside when she noticed two people, who looked a lot like feds, walking up to her studio from a parked black SUV.

"Brittany Garcia," Sandra began. "We're with the FBI. We just want to ask you a few questions about Regis Adams."

Crinkling her brows, Brittany feigned ignorance.

"Who?"

Welsh shot her a look that said, *girl please.*

Turning to walk back inside, she started to shut the door in their faces until she heard the woman's next words.

"You know, I admire your story, Brittany," Sandra said.

"You got out the streets, went to school and even helped make a better life for your brother. It really is too bad he's messing up that good life you've given him."

Hand on the doorknob, Brittany stopped, in place.

"What are you talking about?"

Facing Welsh, Sandra decided to have some fun.

"Oh, Agent Welsh she doesn't know!"

Brittany, who was tired and not happy with the woman's sarcasm was about to cuss her out until the man spoke up.

"I can show you better than I can tell you," said Welsh as he opened an envelope with photos inside, taken by their private investigator. Taking the envelope, Brittany went over them, one by one. By the time she got to the eleventh photo, she had seen enough.

"Listen, we don't want to roll your brother up, he seems like a good kid despite his extracurricular activities, but we will. We hear he's running a full drug operation at his fancy little Ivy League school. Word on campus is he's the go-to guy for any drug and that he works with a high-profile dealer out of New York."

"Tell her the rest, Welsh," Sandra said, egging him on.

Snapping his fingers, Welsh dropped the best part.

"The feds, you know, us, have been trying to get to that high-profile drug dealer out of New York for years!"

Brittany stood silently, knowing she was cornered. Talk, or her brother would be arrested or made to spy and snitch.

"Come inside."

Turning around, she walked into her shop, where the buzzing noise of needles steady at work hummed rhythmically. Instead of taking them to her office, she led them to a meeting space that was farther away from the noise.

"What do you want?" she asked, plopping down into the chair at the head of the table.

"Start with what really happened the night that you

were with Paul Rucker. Particularly the moment when he was shot and killed."

"How about we start with I-m-m-u-n-i-t-y," she spelled out.

Looking at each other, they nodded and motioned for Brittany to continue.

"Oh, unt unt, I know I was in the streets but I'm not there now. I'm going to need that in writing."

Sliding a legal pad across the table to them, Brittany waited for Sandra to pick a pen from the container in the middle of the table and jot down an agreement. Once a note was written, she reviewed it, took a photo and sent it to her attorney to make sure it could be considered legit.

Receiving the green light, Brittany sighed and pushed into the back of her chair. She raised her hand to her temple and closed her eyes. That night was chaotic and her mind raced when she thought about everything that happened. She'd run away from her group home for the second time that month and needed to get some fast money so she could buy a bus ticket for Atlanta. Raised in the system, ever since her mother was slain in a drive-by shooting, the only family she had was her brother, and as soon as she got settled in Atlanta she planned to come back for him.

Calling a friend, she went to a spot where she'd picked up men before, and there she met Paul Rucker for the first time that night. He pointed to her, she walked over to the car and got in. Speeding off, Rucker headed for his favorite area to take hookers, parked and took out a baggie full of coke.

"He just started doing a line and we talked for a little bit. Then…" her voice trailed off.

"Keep going, Brittany."

Frustrated that she had to, once again, relive this time in her life, Brittany took a deep breath and finished her story.

"I went to give him some head when there was a loud thump and the car shook. I, um, accidentally bit Paul's dick, and he jumped up and got out the car to see what was going on."

She stopped for a second, stood, and went to the mini fridge that was in the corner. She grabbed a small bottle of water. Taking a sip, she walked back to her seat.

"There was a man standing outside the car. He was in his fifties maybe, salt and pepper hair, sharp eyebrows and in all black. I said he had on a ski mask, but he didn't, I saw his face," she mumbled. "I didn't know his name at the time but I later found out it was Regis Adams."

"So why did you lie?"

"Because I wanted to live. He said he would let me go, but if I said anything he'd come back for me. So, I lied. A few weeks went by and the guy from that night, the man who killed Paul, came up to me when I was waiting at a bus stop. He drove up and told me to get in. I did, and instead of taking me back to my group home, he drove me to a house in Virginia. Told me he was proud I hadn't said anything and that he wanted to repay me for my silence."

She stopped talking and looked down at her hands, which rested on her lap. Regis had been good to her over the years. In a way, he had saved her and her brother. He'd given them money, advice, a chance at life. Instead of snitching on him Brittany felt like she should be repaying him; but as much as she was grateful to him, she would always put her brother and his well-being, first.

"Will you testify to this?"

"What choice do I have?" However, she knew the answer was none.

CHAPTER 31

SHAKE DOWN

It was Ruby's day off so Vanessa decided to do something she rarely got a chance to do but was great at, cook. Ruby had been in Devin's life for so long that when Vanessa moved in she quickly learned that the older woman was not about to let her come in and change things, including taking over her daily duties with cooking and cleaning. Her off days were the only time Vanessa could truly cater to and show out for her man, and she made sure to remind him that she was a southern woman who could throw down.

Grabbing a skillet, she set out to make her specialty, homemade Crawfish Etouffee with red beans and rice, and cornbread. Turning on some neo soul so she could jam while she worked, she heard the doorbell rang. Not expecting anyone to stop by, she wiped her hands on a nearby kitchen towel and glanced at the front door camera, which was placed in the corner of the kitchen.

"Great," she muttered. "Regis."

Had she not been sure that he'd heard all the noise with

the pots and music, she would have left him standing there and acted like no one was home, but it was too late. Walking through the foyer, she swung the heavy door open with a fake smile already planted on her usually cheery face.

"Vanessa!"

To her dismay, the aging man swung his arms over her body, damn near squeezing the air out of her with his small frame.

"Regis, what are you doing here?"

She hoped her question didn't sound as accusatory as it did to her, and luckily it didn't.

"I was in the area and figured I'd check in on my favorite young couple. Where's Devin? There have been some questions regarding some donors that I want to talk to him about. Know anything about that, Vanessa?"

Eyeing her down, and before waiting for her to invite him in, Regis scooted Vanessa to the right and started walking into the house like he owned the place, taking a seat on the sectional.

Great, she thought, *he knows I've been looking into him.*

"He had a meeting with Darlene, maybe that's what they're discussing. He should be home in about an hour. I was just cooking something for him to eat when he makes it back."

Regis nodded his approval, but Vanessa didn't miss the look of appreciation on his face and she knew it was for more than her cooking skills, as his visual appraisal of her went all the way down to her crotch.

"Devin was smart, getting him a southern woman."

Not sure what to make of his remark, Vanessa decided to excuse herself and head back to the kitchen. She didn't want Regis in her home, especially without Devin present, but she knew sending him away would send alarm bells off in his head and she wanted to give Devin a chance to bring up the donors with him before he got on the defense.

"Well, make yourself at home, you know where everything is. I'll just be in the kitchen."

Bag Lady played in the background as she tried to get back in her zone, but knowing the man whom she despised and had recently determined was a bonified criminal, made it hard. When her cornbread batter was ready to be put in the oven, she bent over to slide it in, but something slid down her backside. Jumping up from her position, she almost spilled the batter, while a smiling Regis stood behind her.

"My, my, my that looks delicious."

Instead of looking at the food, he was looking at her. Immediately, she was fearful about what he was going to do next. Moving her body away from his, she proceeded to put the pan on the rack and quickly stood up to add more space between her and the man she'd come to hate. He began walking towards her to close the space, but the front door swung open and Devin's voice called out.

"Vanessa, I'm home! Where's Regis? I saw his car in the driveway."

Running out of the kitchen, Vanessa took his arrival as God-sent and rushed into his arms.

"Wow baby, are you okay? I was only gone a few hours," laughed Devin.

Walking out of the kitchen behind her, Regis had replaced his menacing smirk that he'd just worn, with a smile.

"Hey, Devin, I was telling Vanessa that I was in the

area and wanted to come by and say hi. I know I should have called first."

"That's okay, I've been meaning to reach out to you anyway."

Still traumatized by what had just happened, or almost happened, Vanessa looked from Devin to Jacob and walked out of the room.

Confused and concerned about what had happened before he arrived, Devin turned to Regis and asked if everything was okay.

"Yeah son, I think she was on a call that upset her before I arrived. Anyway, I'm going to head back out, but happy I got to see you. Before I leave, is there something you want to talk about? You said you've been meaning to reach out."

Devin thought about it but decided it wasn't the right time to broach the subject of Regis's suspicious fundraising tactics on his campaign or any of the other things he'd just recently discovered. Promising Regis that he would schedule a time for them to meet later in the week, Devin rushed the older man out the door. Saying goodbye, he stood at the entrance and watched him drive off. Closing the door, he went upstairs to find a very upset Vanessa pacing the room.

Hearing him enter, she whirled around with red eyes and crossed her arms over her chest.

"He disrespected me, there's no way in hell he's coming back into this house."

Her accent was out in full force, something that only happened when she was really livid. Grabbing her shaking hand, Devin pulled her down to the bed and waited for her to tell him what had happened. For a long moment he looked at Vanessa, and then became scared. *What did Regis do?* He wondered.

"Devin, he walked up on me when I was cooking in the kitchen and put his hand on my back when I was bent over the oven. He was inappropriate and made comments about me being a good woman and said I looked delicious. Well, he said the food looked delicious but he was looking at me when he said it, then licked his lips, and…" For what seemed like ten minutes straight Vanessa talked fast, and with her hands. She was undeniably upset, and all Devin could do was remain quiet and try to process all that she was telling him. Hearing that Regis had made his lady uncomfortable outraged him, but getting upset would only make the situation worse.

Finally, when she took a breath he decided to jump in, but did so cautiously. Placing his hand on the small of her back he slowly massaged the tension he felt in her body.

"Ness, I'm so sorry that happened, baby. I promise I'm going to find out what's going on. You won't have to worry about him coming over here anymore."

Covering her with his arms, Devin was sick with anger. The fact that Regis intentionally triggered Vanessa made Devin want to jump in the car to go find the man and kill him. It was obvious Regis did what he did to knock people off of their game. It seemed like somewhat of a warning to both of them. A reminder of who he was and what he was capable of doing. Not one to assault women, he was a master manipulator who knew what to do to get under people's skin.

Vanessa trembled at Devin's touch. The anger that was already rising was now at its tipping point. Her piercing red eyes brimmed with tears as she threw Devin's arms off of her and moved away from him.

"You know damn well what I've been through and how I was assaulted in college! Get this shit under control, and get it done now."

Grabbing Devin's car keys from the dresser, she walked to the bedroom door and tossed them over the banister.

"Get out of here and go get this evil ass man."

With that, she folded her arms and waited for him to exit the home he had bought and paid for. The home that he paid the mortgage on, and had lived in for years prior to their relationship. Knowing better than to challenge her over that bit of information, Devin smartly knew not to put up a struggle. His naturally good-natured fiancée was rightfully enraged.

"I love you, Vanessa, I'm sorry. I'll fix this."

Once the front door shut behind him, Vanessa collapsed on the bed in a fit of tears.

Traffic was one of his biggest pet peeves and he avoided it at all costs. Typically, the highway wasn't too bad after 7:30 in the evening, but today seemed to be an exception. A sudden thought came to Devin as he passed a billboard. He snapped his fingers in recognition. Rihanna was in town, and the city was going crazy for her show. As he sat in the car, his thoughts shifted to Vanessa and Regis. There was no way he could return home without getting some answers for Vanessa, so he headed straight to Jacob's house and called Julian to meet him there. It was time for the three of them to sit down and discuss the past. Who was Regis? What did they need to do to get away from him?

Traffic finally dispersed, and Devin took the exit for Takoma Park. Pulling into the driveway, he noticed Julian's car, and one he didn't recognize. Since Julian lived closer to their uncle, Devin wasn't surprised he'd made it there first. But he was curious as to who the other car belonged to. Using his personal key to let himself in, Devin stopped in the foyer when he saw Jacob, sitting with his brother, and some man in a wheelchair.

"Hey Devin, come have a seat," said Uncle Jacob. "Your brother just got here not too long ago, so we haven't talked about anything yet."

Taking the seat next to Julian, Devin eyed the man in the wheelchair. He was an older man whom Devin couldn't place. Before he could ask the gentleman who he was, the man simply showed him a badge, leaving Devin to wonder why an FBI agent was sitting at his uncle's table. Not one to beat around the bush or waste time, Welsh began explaining the reason for his visit.

"Devin and Julian, my name is Curtis Welsh, I'm with the FBI and I'm working on your father's case, which has just been reopened. I don't think your father killed Congressman Paul Rucker, I think Regis Adams did, and your uncle has been helping me gather evidence and testimony to prove that."

Sitting up at the mention of his late father, for the first time since entering the room, Devin noticed an air of familiarity about the FBI agent. A lightbulb went off as Devin zeroed in on the man speaking to him.

"Wait, you were at the raid! I remember you because when the feds were stomping over everyone trying to get to my father, you knocked me down but stayed to help me back up."

A small smile crept onto the agent's face.

"Good memory, yes that was me."

"Fill us in here, what do you mean you think Regis killed Rucker?" interrupted Julian, impatiently.

"We have testimony from Brittany Garcia, who was with the congressman before his death. She has gone on the record and is willing to testify that it was Regis she saw shoot and kill Paul Rucker that day."

"Why is she speaking up now after all these years?" asked Julian angrily.

Welsh went on to explain the circumstances and the additional evidence they had against Regis. Jacob, who'd heard everything already, watched Julian and Devin and waited for their response. Hearing about Jacob's conversation with their father before he died heated Julian up.

"So, you knew all of this but never said anything? To nobody? What, you scared of that old punk ass nigga?" he roared, slamming his fist on the table.

Jacob sat ashamed. He very well could have come forward a long time ago, but it just didn't seem possible.

"Jules, I know you probably don't want to hear this right now, but hell yeah I was scared."

Pausing, he looked at the brothers. They were grown men now but at one time they were boys whom he helped raise.

"When your father first brought Regis around I knew he was bad news. I tried to tell your dad, but he didn't want to listen. I noticed he was getting deeper and deeper into whatever Regis was in, but he would never share details with me. He'd always say stuff like, 'I don't want to involve you in this side of the business. I need you to always be clean in case you need to step up for my boys and Brenda.' He made it clear that he wanted my help in looking after you all, so when he died, and it was clear Regis had something to do with it. I had two choices: go to the police with my little bit of evidence and risk your safety or keep things to myself and watch all of our backs moving forward. I did the latter until your car accident, Devin."

"It was Regis?" asked Devin, who had finally stopped staring daggers at his uncle. He understood the spot Uncle Jacob had been put in and appreciated his protection for all those years.

"It was," Jacob said. "I don't know who he got to tamper with the car, but I know he orchestrated it in order to send a message to me. He was telling me that if I shared any information about him with the authorities, he would kill you."

Sitting back in his chair, Devin looked at Julian, who had his arms crossed and a scowl on his face. He hadn't forgiven Uncle Jacob yet for his failure to step up and stop Regis after all those years, but at this point he knew the focus needed to be on ending Regis for good.

Jumping back in the conversation, Welsh wrapped up the meeting.

"I may call on any or all of you to help pin Regis down. Do you have any questions or concerns about that?"

The three men shook their heads, no.

"Before we leave for the night there's one more thing," said Devin. "My fiancée discovered some more information about Regis and his affiliations based on some donors he's been bringing to my campaign. I can share her notes with you, maybe some of those names can help the case."

Nodding his head in agreement, Welsh looked around and made eye contact with each man at the table. Their anger superseded any flicker of fear, and Welsh knew they all wanted Regis behind bars or dead. It was time to close this chapter.

CHAPTER 32

VALID CONCERNS

Stifling a yawn, Vanessa blinked several times before slowly moving her gaze to the clock hanging on the wall. She absently patted the space next to her, and the emptiness reminded her of the argument she'd had with Devin. He had come home late last night and left early this morning. With a groan, she sat upright and guided her feet into the slippers that lay next to her bed.

Grabbing her phone off the nightstand, she stretched her body and headed for the kitchen. The house had a quirky stillness to it. A nearby lawnmower hummed so loud that the décor around the house slightly shook. It was a beautiful 85-degree summer day, and Vanessa hoped Devin would be home soon so they could talk. Grabbing a quick cup of coffee from the Keurig, she settled down on a bar stool and began to think about the night before. As a replay of her conversation with Devin ran through her mind, the phone rang. On the other end was her sister, Taryn.

"Vanessa, are you okay?"

Hearing her sister's voice immediately calmed her. Taryn had just woken up to Vanessa's text and decided to call her immediately.

"Not really, remember what I told you about Regis? Well, I was right. The other day he came by the house unannounced when Devin wasn't here and he pushed up on me when I was in the kitchen cooking. He made me so uncomfortable, sis, all I could remember was when…"

Before she could finish her sentence, tears welled in her eyes and she looked away. Sitting on the other end of the phone, an angry Taryn knew what she was referring to.

"When Daniel assaulted you."

Looking out the window, all Vanessa could do was nod. For a moment she was taken back to the night of graduation when she'd decided to go out and celebrate.

Her family had traveled back to Texas right after graduation so Vanessa decided to spend a night out with former classmates. After a night of drinks at a graduation party, Vanessa and her group of friends drunkenly called their Ubers. Daniel, a friend since freshman year of college, and Vanessa lived in the same building so they decided to share an Uber to go home. Once there, the two stumbled out of the car and Daniel walked Vanessa to her apartment, on the first floor. Reaching for her keys, she opened the door. When she went to tell Daniel goodnight, he pushed past her and walked inside the unit. Laughing at him, Vanessa figured he was just being goofy and was just a little too buzzed.

"Go home, Dan, it's four in the morning, and I need

some sleep."

Daniel turned towards Vanessa, and before she knew it he was on top of her, pinning her arms to her sides. Screaming for him to stop, he unbuttoned his jeans and proceeded to rape Vanessa. As soon as he left, she cried quietly and headed for the shower. The water was hot, but the need to scrub every inch of her body made it necessary. She went between washcloth to loofah, trying her best to rid her body of the scent that permeated her every being. The water cascaded down her sides and the smell of sex erupted her senses.

Holed up in her apartment, barely bathing for days, Vanessa had fallen into a deep depression. The spunk she typically had was now nonexistent and the light in her eyes was gone. For two months, she barely ate, and it showed. The job she'd landed prior to graduation was given to someone else when she failed to show up for work on the first day, and as she listened to the voicemail from the hiring manager telling her the news, all she could do was cry into the couch pillows. Sitting up from her fetal position, she reluctantly returned one of her sister's many calls, and told her what had happened.

Taryn, who had been worried about her sister for some time, jumped on the first flight as soon as Vanessa shared that she has been sexually assaulted. What she saw brought her to tears, and when Vanessa cried in her arms about the boy who'd violated her, Taryn wanted to fight. Resisting the urge to find the person responsible for hurting her sister, Taryn focused her attention on nursing her back to health. She held her hand the day they went to the police station to report Daniel, and again on the way home. Although a report was submitted, nothing ever came of it. Officers suggested it was too late to report the rape, especially since a rape kit was never administered. Regardless, taking that step helped restore some confidence in Vanessa, and with the help of Taryn and a new therapist, she was on the mend within the month. Eventually she learned to embrace sex again, and by the time she met Devin, Vanessa was open to sexual exploration.

"I'm so sorry, Vanessa, is there anything I can do?" asked Taryn.

Letting off a sigh, Vanessa just wanted to forget about Regis. After telling her no, the two stayed on the phone for a little longer, discussing the upcoming bachelorette party. Finally, Vanessa snuggled up under her weighted blanket and tried to take her mind off of Regis. Midway through *Waiting to Exhale*, some keys jingled and Devin gingerly walked through the door. He hoped Vanessa would be in a better mood than she had been the night before, especially after he shared an update with her.

Devin walked cautiously towards the couch and bent down to kiss a stoic Vanessa on the forehead. Sitting up with her legs crossed, she waited for him to share the latest news. Going through each detail, Devin gave her the full rundown and didn't leave anything out. Similar to how he and Julian reacted the night before, Vanessa was angry and ready for war.

CHAPTER 33

UNWANTED ADVANCE

Slamming on his brakes, Julian narrowly missed the back of a Camry that had just cut him off. Julian expertly switched lanes to avoid being behind the car, which donned a North Carolina license plate. It was obvious the driver wasn't up to par on the unwritten rules of navigating through traffic, and Julian wanted no part of an accident.

Thinking back to the meeting at Uncle Jacob's the night before, he grew upset. How had all those years gone by without Regis being held accountable for the shit he pulled? Swerving into the next lane, his phone rang and Avery's name popped up. Using his Bluetooth, he answered and smiled as the sound of her voice came through. That alone always calmed him down.

"Hey baby, what are you doing?" she cooed.

Exhaling loudly instead of responding, Julian laughed.

"Must be in traffic. Well, if I move out there at least I won't have to adjust to that. L.A. has already prepared me."

"About that…"

On her side, Avery stopped patting her growing belly and immediately thought the worst.

"Julian, I thought there wouldn't be any games this time," she started.

"Baby, no I promise it's not that. There's some wild stuff going on with Regis, and the FBI just reopened my dad's case. There's a lot to tell, but I'm too exhausted by it all. Can I call you back once I make it home? Promise to tell you everything then."

"Of course, and drive safe. I love you."

Hanging up, Julian blasted Kendrick Lamar's latest album and drowned out his thoughts with good music until he was in his neighborhood. Parking his silver Audi beside his Lambo, he walked into his building and headed straight to his condominium so he could undress and shower. Too tired to call Avery back, he sent her a text promising to call the next day and was about to pass out when he felt a hand reach inside his boxers. Jumping up, Julian turned on the lights, and standing there in all her naked glory, was Jade.

"What the fuck! How did you get in here?" he demanded.

Ignoring his question, she walked towards him with a deranged look on her face.

"I've missed you."

Eyes wide, Julian was scared for his life. This was some shit out of, *A Thin Line Between Love and Hate.*

"I've moved on, Jade, I told you this. You need to leave."

Grinning, like he had not just dismissed her, Jade stopped walking towards him and headed back to the bed.

"Come on it's late, let's just lay down."

Mouth wide open in shock, Julian was convinced she was delusional and dangerous. Grabbing his gun from the nightstand, he raised it up to her and told her once again to get out. Facing Julian and the shiny Glock, Jade began to slowly pick up her clothes. Julian angrily waited until she was fully dressed and walking out the door. To make sure she'd truly leave the premises he followed her downstairs and watched as she walked to the corner of the street to meet what he assumed was a rideshare. When she was out of his line-of-sight Julian went back upstairs, called security to alert them about Jade, then double checked all the locks and alarms before lying back down. However, by this time he was too scared to close his eyes and sleep.

First thing the next morning, he jumped up to go to the police station. Something told him he needed a restraining order. Now, not only did he have Regis, but his ex-fling was also something to worry about. Thoughts of asking Avery to move in with him left his mind, now was not the time to have her around this drama.

CHAPTER 34

GIRL'S WEEKEND

Bags were packed and waiting at the front door. Not one to like big group trips, Vanessa wondered how her three-day weekend, bachelorette experience with ten girls was going to go, but the timing was perfect and she wanted to rid her mind of all things Regis. Wearing a pair of dark shades, she made sure she wasn't forgetting anything. The flight to Montego Bay, Jamaica was close to four hours long and all she wanted to do was sleep on the plane. Her phone sounded in the pocket of her oversized cardigan, and as she looked down to read it, she smiled when she saw the name.

Taryn: Sis, are you ready for your weekend? Can't wait until you get here! Let me know as soon as you board the plane.

Vanessa: Thanks T, the driver just got here, I'll see you soon.

Just as the doorbell rang, with the driver ready to take her to Baltimore-Washington International airport, Vanessa felt some strong arms grab her into a warm hug.

"Have fun this weekend, baby, but not too much. I need you to come back to me."

Enjoying his touch, Vanessa, closed her eyes for a second before promising not to do anything too naughty. Interrupted by the sound of the doorbell, the two turned their attention toward the front door.

Releasing each other's arms, Devin opened the door to meet Landon, Vanessa's driver since the start of the campaign. Taking one last mental inventory of all she'd packed, Vanessa felt everything was good to go. She slung her large Telfar bag over her shoulder, and the three of them headed out to the car, bogged down by all of Vanessa's luggage. Once everything was loaded, Vanessa met Devin with one last hug and a peck on the lips.

"I love you," she whispered, huskily.

"Girl, get out of here before I make you miss your flight."

As she giggled and stepped into the town car, Devin could only smile.

"I'll see you Monday, baby," he called to her open window.

Vanessa nodded, wishing for a second that it wasn't too late to cancel the trip. If it weren't for Taryn and Mikayla pressuring her to have a bachelorette weekend, plus Darlene pushing the idea as an editorial for the campaign, she would have just chosen to have an intimate girl's night out.

The car ride was short but sweet, and the arrival to the private jet that awaited her at the hangar brought tears to her eyes. Taryn really went all out for the weekend.

After thanking Landon and speaking with the pilots,

Vanessa leaned back into the comfortable reclining seat. Even though the flight attendant brought her a flute of champagne before take-off, by the time the plane was in the air, Vanessa was sound asleep with the full glass sitting next to her. Sleep was good, because for 72 hours straight she would be up and running through an island with a bunch of women.

Approaching the mansion, she felt another sense of nausea when she thought about the group of girls who would accompany her for the weekend. Though she loved everyone who'd traveled to celebrate with her, the thought of being coddled and showered with attention was unnerving for Vanessa, who typically shied away from receiving what she'd consider to be too much attention. To take her mind off of the coming festivities, she took a moment to admire the beautiful landscaping and massive grounds surrounding the large home. Before she could exit the car, Taryn, followed by Mikayla, burst through the front doors wearing bright smiles and colorful sundresses. Seeing their faces and drunken smiles made her relax.

Within minutes, Vanessa was given a Lemon Drop shot and her belongings were picked up and delivered to the master suite by the staff hired for the weekend. This was sure to be the bachelorette party to rival all, and Vanessa felt her anxiety subside. It wasn't until she'd downed her shot, and said hello to the other girls, that she noticed her cousin, who hadn't been at the crawfish boil when they were in Houston recently, walking into the room. Brandy was that one cousin Vanessa had grown up with and only tolerated because she was family. Annoyed that her sister had invited their crazy ass cousin, Brandy, Vanessa made a mental note to cuss Taryn out when they were alone.

"Hey cuz," Brandy said in her southern drawl. Reaching for a hug, her massive breasts, which were always front and center, crushed Vanessa.

"This a nice ass house, cuz."

Vanessa cringed, not just at what she said, but because her breath smelled of Newport's and weed. Seeing the look on her sister's face, Taryn hurried between them, handing Brandy a drink.

"Come on y'all, let's go get dressed for tonight," Taryn said.

The bass blared, and the words to Chris Brown's latest song rang out across the nightclub. Even in Jamaica, the song was a hit. The place was packed, and the lively group of women enjoyed the party from just a few feet away of the dancefloor, in a section reserved especially for them. Stocked with alcohol and food, they had everything they needed within reach.

Before she became a stylist, Taryn performed as a trained dancer. Moving her body to the beat, she blended in with the music. Taking a moment to melt into the sounds, she grabbed her sister up from the lounge chair and they danced side-by-side. Feeling like a couple of schoolgirls, they giggled and kept dancing until night became morning.

"Now that was a good time," said Brandy as they poured

into one of the three vehicles waiting for them outside the club. Unfortunately for Vanessa, her cousin was riding in the car with her, Taryn and Mikayla while the rest of the girls piled into the remaining cars. The entire ride back, Brandy, who'd had her share of Rum Punch, talked so much that the driver tried drowning her out with loud music. His attempts were unsuccessful.

"Yeah, but I don't know about your friends. They a little too stuck up for me," she said, pointing towards Mikayla who was sitting in the front row. Holding her compact up to her face as she fixed her lipstick, Mikayla could see Brandy's finger pointed at her through the mirror's reflection.

"You're low vibrational," she responded without turning around. Shutting her compact and placing it in her purse, she continued. "Low class, bitch. Can't take you nowhere."

Mikayla was no pushover and had had enough of her friends' cousin. If needed, she was ready to give Brandy a proper ass kicking, Brooklyn style.

Lifting her hand, Brandy went to grab Mikayla, but was intercepted by Taryn's quick reflexes. Yanking Brandy's hand back into her lap, Taryn felt her blood boiling. It was only the first night and her patience with the girl was waning. Refusing to put up with their cousin's attitude for the whole weekend and letting it ruin Vanessa's bachelorette, she gave her an ultimatum.

"Stop starting shit," Taryn said in her ear. "We don't need you creating drama this weekend. Nip this in the bud now or take your ass home tomorrow. I'm happy to organize a flight home for you."

Brandy twisted her face in anger. Aware that her cousin was trying to throw her off the trip, she had a few choice words for her.

"Ever since we were kids y'all have acted like you were better than everybody, but baby you and Vanessa can still get that ass tapped. Only reason I came on this trip is because my mama wanted me to."

Vanessa rolled her eyes. Noticing this, Taryn grew more upset. She should have never let her mother talk her into inviting Brandy in the first place. Dating back to their childhood years, Brandy had always had a knack for bringing drama and problems into every situation.

Pulling up to the house, Taryn decided to leave the conversation for later. This weekend was for Vanessa and her job was to maintain good energy and keep fun activities coming, and she was determined to make sure everything went smoothly.

And for the next three days, the trip went smoother than Taryn had even hoped. Brandy, who nursed a hangover from the Rum Punches, became more reclusive, to everyone's satisfaction. Between the beautiful home they'd rented with the outdoor amenities: pool, hot tub, sauna, and so much more, and the delicious food they'd had prepared by a Jamaican chef, the group walked around happy, relaxed and chill. Vanessa was happy that Taryn hadn't booked activities on the island for them back-to-back, and had allotted time for some rest and relaxation. Grabbing a tennis racket, she went downstairs to meet Brandy, who had been surprisingly quiet and reserved since the first night. The day before, the group went zip-ling, and on the way back to the house she'd mentioned seeing Vanessa on the tennis court that morning, and had asked for some lessons.

Taking some towels, they walked down to the court.

The weather was perfect for some outdoor exercise, and for a minute, they just stood around enjoying the views and sunshine. For about 45 minutes Vanessa showed her cousin a few basic moves, and before the end of the lesson Brandy was able to serve the ball across the net with a form that was shocking for most beginners. Vanessa wasn't surprised, her cousin had always been athletic, landing a scholarship for track & field to Prairie View A&M University. An accident during her junior year derailed her track goals, but she was still able to finish school and land a job as a physical therapist. Grabbing some water, the girls, who were raised as sisters but barely had anything to talk about, now just sat quietly. Eyes closed, Brandy raised her hands and stretched towards the sky.

"I really am sorry how I acted after the club," said Brandy, with her eyes still closed. "I was a little drunk and my jealousy came out, I guess. And I got a lot going on back home."

"Why are you jealous?"

Opening her eyes, she faced Vanessa.

"Come on, you know why. You and Taryn have gone on to really do great things and my life hasn't really gone anywhere. Three kids with different dads, and none of them pay child support or are around. I don't know, at one point it seemed like I had it all together, and then, bam, I didn't. It's been a struggle."

"Oh, Brandy, we all got some shit going on. Not everything is perfect, don't let social media fool you."

For a second Vanessa thought about the times she had questioned if her fiancé was satisfied with just being with her and not another man or woman. Even though Devin seemed content with just her, sometimes she wondered if he really was, which is why she'd suggested they bring partners into their bedroom. Vanessa would never tell Devin this, but she was secretly happy that they weren't able to go through with the idea, even though it was hers to begin with.

Aside from her relationship, there were also the instances when she'd accidentally read comments online or heard a journalist on television critiquing her. More seriously, people didn't know about the noose that was mailed to their home, the nasty things said to them at events when security was too lax, or the wickedness of politics, like the situation with Regis.

"Look at you. You're beautiful. After three babies you still have a track star body, and you've got a great job. If you're not happy now, what will make you happy?"

Thinking for a second, Brandy smiled.

"Always wanted to coach, but with three kids, a coaching salary just ain't enough."

Grabbing her hand and lifting her up from the bench, Vanessa placed an arm across her cousin's shoulders and the two walked back up the hill towards the house.

"Let's think of something, maybe it can be an initiative that can be tied to the Isaiah Barrett Foundation. Papa would have loved some type of physical activities in our communities."

Hugging her cousin, Brandy was happy her mother had talked her into coming.

"Now, can we talk about you coming up with a wedding hashtag? I can't believe you don't have one yet," said Brandy, switching the conversation.

CHAPTER 35

THE SITUATION ROOM

Gathered in a large conference room, Sandra clapped her hands.

"We have the evidence to finally get him. Jacob has turned over Thaddeus's recordings and Brittany submitted a sworn affidavit. All that is left, is to get a confession."

"But with what we have already do we really need a confession?"

"Agent Welsh, I told you I wanted a slam dunk here. We need to bury Regis this time around."

Looking around the room, she continued.

"The nail in the coffin needs to come from Devin. Get Regis to admit to having his father killed, to the shady donors, to everything. It appears he's made some side deals with a few disreputable businesses and untrustworthy politicians, on Devin's behalf, to set him up. His shifty involvement on this campaign is minor considering his impressive criminal history, but it could be the last big piece we need to nail him."

"I understand boss, you're right. I'll reach out to Devin."

Sitting in his office at the campaign headquarters, Devin waited for Regis to arrive. Worried about how the conversation would unfold, and fearing the worst, he glanced down nervously at the silver pen that lay absently on his desk. The FBI was well aware of how careful Regis was, which was evident in how long he'd been able to get away with his transgressions, but they still planted the listening device in Devin's office in case Regis slipped up and admitted to anything criminal.

Devin jumped at the loud buzzing noise. Answering the intercom, his assistant informed him that Regis had arrived. On edge, but trying his best to look composed, Devin stood to greet the man whom he had once looked at with so much adoration and respect. Tempted to take his first and punch him square in the mouth for all he'd put his family through, Devin quickly placed his hands in his pockets instead. He would stand to appear cordial, but would not shake the man's hand. That would be going too far.

"Thanks for coming by," he started.

"When have I ever not shown up when you've called?"

Ignoring his attempt to connect with him, Devin took his seat. Instead of beating around the bush, he decided to get straight to the point. Pulling out the notes Vanessa had uncovered, detailing the donors, Devin tossed them across the desk for Regis to view. Scanning the list, Regis chuckled.

"Vanessa really is thorough," he taunted, looking Devin in the eye. "I've always told you, you've got a good one."

Slamming his fist on the table, Devin sprang to his feet.

No longer able to hold in his real emotions, he dove ahead full force and laid it all out.

"What the fuck have you done, man? I know that somehow you had my dad killed, I know you killed Paul Rucker. You intentionally made Vanessa uncomfortable, tried to kill me in an accident and then you try to get me involved in some illegal shit that could cause me to lose the election and get thrown in jail. Why?"

Legs crossed, Regis sat back and watched Devin explode. He was mildly amused, as it seemed to remind him of the time when Devin's father, Thaddeus, got upset with him during his visit to see him in jail.

"Those are all lies," he said simply.

"Bullshit!"

"Where are the receipts, Devin? The proof? You have none because none of what you've just accused me of is true."

"Brittany Garcia," said Devin succinctly and without explanation.

Outside, in the FBI truck, the team couldn't believe that Devin had fallen so far off script and was sharing all of this information. Still hoping to get something on the wire, Sandra instructed the team to hold their positions and not move in. Ignoring Devin's mention of the woman identified as the sole witness to Congressman Rucker's murder, she listened as Regis continued.

"Devin, I've always wanted what was best for you and your brother. I've been there for you both ever since you lost your father. I know this campaign has you a little stressed out so I'm going to give you a pass today, but don't let this happen again."

Rising to his feet, Regis faced a visibly outraged Devin for a few more seconds before he looked down at the silver pen, smirked, and walked out the door.

Outside, the team felt defeated. They had enough to arrest Regis, but they wanted to make sure it was enough to put him away for a long time. While the team of agents disbanded, Sandra and Welsh reconvened. The fact that Regis had been able to get away with murder and corruption for so long made them cognizant of the fact that he probably had moles within the FBI. Aware of this possibility, the two hadn't let the others know that they had instructed Devin to mention Brittany's name in order to gauge Regis's reaction. To their delight, Regis had taken the bait, because as soon as Brittany was mentioned, he got up to leave. Certain that he was headed in the direction of her shop, Sandra and Welsh jetted off towards Tattoo Inc.

On the way there, after calling for backup, Welsh phoned Ian, who had been anxiously waiting for this story to break.

"Ian, don't plan on going to sleep tonight, we almost have him and you will be the first to know."

On the other end of the line, Ian Thompson stood up from his desk and began pacing. *Is this story finally going to have a proper ending?* he asked himself.

Hanging up, Welsh felt a rush of excitement and fear. On one hand he felt relief at the prospect of closing a long chapter, on the other hand he hoped they wouldn't be too late to save Brittany, unlike the many others who hadn't survived the wrath of Regis Adams.

CHAPTER 36

ANOTHER ONE

Brittany had finally finished with her last client for the day. Grabbing her coat and collecting her belongings, she turned off the lights and stepped outside to close up for the night. Walking to her car, the street was quiet, but something in the air made a chill go down her spine. Looking around the garage, she saw cars scattered in different spots, and nothing looked out of the ordinary. Rushing to unlock her car door, she threw her things in the passenger seat and slid behind the wheel. Safely out of the garage and on the road, she let out a small laugh at her paranoia. Although she felt lighter after coming clean about what really happened to the Congressman, she was scared of Regis finding out and coming after her, as he had done to Paul Rucker.

Stopping at a red light, she reached for the volume control on her radio to turn up the music, then glanced at her glove compartment where she kept her gun. *I'm being ridiculous, of course it's still in there*, she thought silently. *I don't know, maybe I should double check just to make sure.* Just as her hand moved to look, she felt cold steel on the right side of her face, and went numb. Behind her, a voice spoke low and evenly.

"Looking for this? When this light turns green make a left and turn into that alley."

"Regis, no!" yelled Brittany, recognizing the voice immediately. Tears came and her hands trembled on the steering wheel.

"I should have killed you all those years ago. I thought a hood rat like you would appreciate a second chance at life and would keep your mouth shut. I was wrong, so now, here we are."

"They threatened my brother, what was I supposed to do! Regis, it's not too late, I can just tell them I lied, I'll do that and..."

"But it is too late," he interjected.

In an alley far from street view, Brittany parked her car. Regis reached forward, gripping his hands around her neck. Squeezing until her eyes were shut, he prepared to suffocate her.

Then feeling his fingers move from around her neck, Brittany opened her eyes in confusion.

Just as he'd felt the need to handle Paul Rucker on his own, instead of hiring someone to take him out, Regis had felt it necessary to personally see to it that Brittany took her last breath.

"Look what I have," he said instead, shaking a plastic bottle with a sneer. "I figure it best we keep things simple this go-around. I'm too old now to try and move a body or clean up. This will have to do."

Dumping a handful of pills into her hand, he handed

her a flat bottle of Sprite from her cupholder and told her to eat up.

"Those little blue tablets are going to help me do the job."

"I don't know what these are, I'm not taking them."

Grabbing the back of her neck again, Regis pulled Brittany close to his face until his breath was on her brow.

"Take the damn pills, bitch."

Crying, Brittany began filling her mouth. As she was reaching for the bottle of Sprite to wash them down, bright lights appeared from behind them and sirens sounded from all directions.

"Shit!" shouted Regis, slapping the back of her seat. Before Brittany could spit the pills out, Regis lunged forward and clamped his hand around her mouth, causing her to gag and choke.

"All you had to do was keep your damn mouth shut. Wasn't I good to you, girl!"

Shaking underneath his hold, Brittany tried nodding her head in agreement but was unable to do that and keep from swallowing the pills. Before either of them could decide their next steps, glass shattered around them as a bullet shot from the distance crashed through a window. Everything that happened afterwards was a blur.

CHAPTER 37

A NEW DAY

Leaves blew past the window as the season changed to Fall. Ian Thompson was cleaning out his desk, whistling as he packed up. Later that evening the *The Daily Sun* was throwing him a retirement party in his honor. For weeks he'd been receiving recognition and awards for his reporting on Regis Adams and the man's involvement in the framing of Thaddeus Simmons, the murder of Congressman Paul Rucker and his many criminal activities throughout the years. After an impressive career in journalism and investigative reporting, he was leaving on his terms, and he'd never felt better.

Now, Charles Welsh went to work every day and had a new lease on life. Every time the elevator went past the fourth floor he smiled and felt vindicated. Following the arrest of Regis Adams, Welsh was promoted and moved to Sandra's division. He was the happiest he'd been in years, and the bureau was considering both him and Sandra for a commendation.

For the first time in years, Congressman Paul Rucker's family felt at peace as they were able to finally put together the last pieces to the puzzle. Since day one they were unconvinced that it had been Thaddeus who killed Paul. Now, they were able to fully move on.

Brittany Garcia was relieved. After the unsuccessful attempt on her life, she'd resumed living and for the first time, felt free. Grateful that she was able to keep her brother safe, Brittany decided to make some changes, and had since joined a church and gotten baptized. She was ready for something new and pure. Once her brother was made aware of what his sister had gone through to keep him safe, he retired early from the drug game, promising to make better choices so that Brittany's sacrifices weren't made in vain.

At Jacob's house, a very happy group of six sat around the television screen and celebrated. Regis had just been indicted on 24 federal counts, including wide-ranging racketeering conspiracy charges, fraud, money laundering, bribery, manslaughter and more, and justice felt like it was finally being served.

Jacob felt at peace for the first time since losing his best friend, and although they had a while to go with the trial and sentencing, the Simmons family got the closure and peace they'd been searching for since the day Thaddeus died. Ever since news of the high-profile arrest was made public, people were coming forward with stories of blackmail and extortion that they'd also received at the hands of Regis Adams. Reports were flooding in and interviews of scorned politicians and businessmen were broadcasted across news stations. Republicans and Democrats came together for one day of celebration before returning to their opposite corners.

One surprising moment came when the mother and son from Devin's car accident filed charges against Regis, upon learning of his role in their near-death experience. A member from Devin's security detail had come forward and admitted to tampering with the car after being threatened and extorted by Regis. It looked like they would get a payday after all, and at Regis's expense.

"Avery, pass the popcorn. They're about to show him doing the walk of shame again," said Vanessa.

"Girl, go and grab another bag."

Looking down at her stomach, Avery rubbed her protruding belly and smiled.

"You know I'm eating for two."

Darlene walked in the room, beaming.

"Devin, campaign donations are through the roof! I think Regis's arrest helped to make you the sure winner, and listen to this, Jada Pinkett reached out. She wants you and the entire family to be guests on her show, *Red Table Talk*, after the election!"

Vanessa sat up straight at this information.

"Jada Pinkett? Devin, you've been getting calls for interviews from all of the major media outlets, but this could be the one. Plus, she's from Baltimore."

Vanessa's obvious excitement made Darlene happy. With Vanessa's support, it wouldn't be hard to convince Devin that it would be a good idea.

"Let's not get too excited. We need to finish strong and focus on what's next. There's still the debate and our wedding," winked Devin.

"I might as well stay in town for that, flying is getting

uncomfortable," said Avery. "I still have three months to go but I'm ready for maternity leave now."

Following Regis's arrest, Julian opened up to her about everything that had been going on. It didn't take long for her to decide to fly back to the east coast and check on him.

Rubbing her belly, Julian smiled and shook his head in agreement.

"I like that idea."

In Connecticut, Brendan, the son of former Governor Gregory Nichols watched the same news coverage and was not pleased. There was no fanfare, popcorn or laughs. For decades, Regis had been one of the faces of his father's operation, now his, and having him out of commission and locked up posed a major problem to his business.

Having started the bribery ring following his first term as Governor, Greg Nichols decided to get out of the spotlight and remain in the shadows. Following his father's death, nine years earlier, Brendan, a Venture Capitalist, was tasked with keeping the criminal operation going. *I can't believe Regis never told us that the hooker saw him,* he said to himself. *He should have just killed her along with Rucker.* Concerned about what Regis being in custody and questioned by the FBI, could mean for his enterprise, Brendan's mind raced.

Similar in age, he'd known Regis his entire life and had been jealous of the bond he'd shared with his late father. Whenever Brendan complained about their relationship, Governor Nichols would calm him down by saying, "No need to be jealous, son, I like Regis but he's just a boy I took out of the ghetto and prettied up real nice. If anything were to go wrong, he's the one who will go down first. Think of him as the fall guy."

Turning off the television screen, Brendan stood up to make a call. He knew what he needed to do to protect everything his father had built.

CHAPTER 38

OOH BABY

The day of the wedding, Avery woke up with a start. Baby Simmons was doing cartwheels in her belly, making her presence known, and Avery could no longer find a comfortable position to sleep in. Julian left Avery in their suite a couple hours earlier to join Devin and the groomsmen in the penthouse, and she fully intended to enjoy the time alone. At thirty weeks, she appreciated quiet time, and before things got crazy, she just wanted a nice breakfast and a warm bath. The wedding would be an all-day event, and Avery became anxious just thinking about how busy it would be.

Eleven a.m. came quickly, and it was time to get ready for the ceremony.

A knock at the door signaled the arrival of her makeup artist, Bria, who according to her watch was about forty minutes too early. Rising from the sofa to answer the door, she swung it open without looking through the peephole and was surprised to see a woman who wasn't Bria standing in front of her. Before she could react, Avery was pushed back into the room and the woman closed the door behind her. Grabbing the red wig off her head and tossing it on the couch, black curls fell around the woman's shoulders. A light went off and Avery looked on in horror as she recognized the intruder.

"Jade?" she asked, in disbelief.

"Girl, don't ask me no questions, that's my job," said Jade angrily. "Now sit the fuck down, it's time we have a little girl chat."

Pushing Avery onto the couch, Jade began pacing the room.

"You're the reason me and Julian aren't together," she said with wild eyes. "You fucked up my relationship and I know it was you who made him get a restraining order against me!"

Jumping up, Avery moved towards Jade with her hands in the air.

"A what? I had no idea."

"Liar!" screamed Jade, slapping Avery across the face so hard she almost fell back onto the glass table placed in front of the couch. But it was true, Julian had confided in her about Regis but had never said anything about Jade or a restraining order.

Holding onto the corner of the couch before she hit the sharp edges of the table, Avery grabbed hold of her stomach, in pain, and walked towards the kitchen. Steadying her body against the counter, fear turned to anger as she thought back to the abortion she'd gotten following the fight she'd had with Julian's old bitch in college. Grabbing a knife that lay in the sink, which she had used at breakfast, Avery lunged towards Jade with the force of a category five hurricane, catching her off guard. Just as the knife was about to be forced into the side of Jade's neck, the door flew open and Mikayla, Vanessa's best friend, stood there, along with hotel staff. Seeing the action happening in the hotel suite, Mikayla flew inside and tackled Jade before the knife could reach the woman's neck.

A few minutes earlier, Mikayla had taken the elevator up to the 11th floor with a woman with red hair. Mikayla had recognized the woman, but couldn't place her. Exiting, she made it to her door before a light went off. The woman in the lift had been Julian's date at his birthday party, the one who had acted insecure and possessive. Even with the wig, Mikayla was sure it was her. Running to call for hotel security, she met the manager outside of room 1114 just before they heard screaming and something crash to the floor. Using a key to gain access, the manager opened the door, with Mikayla pushing past him to break up the altercation between Jade and a very pregnant and angry Avery.

Breathing deeply, Avery dropped the knife and sat down in the nearest chair, clutching her stomach.

"Are you okay?" asked the hotel manager, kneeling down to Avery's side.

Unable to speak any words, she could only try to call out in distress.

While Mikayla continued restraining Jade, who was unstable and couldn't be trusted, the manager lifted Avery into his arms, rushing her to the elevator. Arriving in the lobby, he flew past the front desk, instructing them to call the police and direct them to Julian Simmons' room. Within half an hour Avery was in a hospital bed with a team of medical professionals surrounding her.

CHAPTER 39

RED TABLE TALK

Reagan Barbara Simmons, named after Avery's paternal grandmother, came into the world weighing 5 pounds and 11 ounces, on October 24th, with a head full of hair. Born premature, Reagan spent her first two months in the NICU, but was finally home with mom and dad. Mom, after enduring countless hours of labor and delivery, with a sea of complications, was healing well, and Julian was waiting on her both hand and foot. For the last couple of months he had refused to leave Avery's side. Even though Jade had been arrested and was now in psychiatric care, Julian regretted not being there the day of the encounter, and vowed to never put Avery in danger again. Avery knew he had good intentions, but was feeling smothered. This was why, when Julian was invited to participate in Devin's *Red Table Talk* interview in New York, she strongly encouraged him to go.

Standing backstage with his mother and sister-in-law Vanessa, Julian faced a mounted screen where a video clip of the day Devin won the election, played. Devin sat in the studio, smiling at the same footage, reminiscing about that special day.

News stations crowded on the lawn of Devin's campaign headquarters, a stately building that housed the biggest news of the night. Reporters were assembled in various locations. Each waiting to be the first to deliver the results of the election season. Commentators filled the silence by making predictions, which did nothing but make voters more anxious. Out of nowhere, a voice yelled out, "Turn that volume up, they have the results!"

On cue, the television volume was turned to the highest octave as the anchor excitedly faced the camera.

"The votes are in and with a historic win, Devin Simmons will now be the next Senator for Maryland!"

With a head slightly bowed and shoulders violently shaking, it was clear Senator-Elect Simmons had become emotional upon hearing the results. His striped tie hung between his legs, which adorned wrinkled slacks; evidence of his lack of sleep during the final days leading to Election Day. Crowds of supporters patted Devin on the back, and a nearby videographer captured his every moment. After months of campaigning, the young senator elected to Congress had proven to the nation that he was mature and well-rounded enough to lead an entire state and represent his country. A sweet scent leaning over his shoulder struck his nostrils and filled him with energy.

"Stand up, baby, and celebrate with us," whispered his wife in her sultry voice. "This is the moment we've been waiting for. We won."

As if a newfound energy had taken over him, the well-groomed, yet tired looking politician, stood to his feet with a confidence that erupted more cheers from the crowd.

His fist pump sent the room into a frenzy and it was then that he noticed the cameras surrounding him. The results were broadcasted live around the world. Baring the dimpled smile he had become known for since his early political career days, Devin stood up, reached out to embrace his new wife, and inched towards his spot at the microphone.

Thinking about all that had happened to get him to this moment, for a second, he stood upright and marveled at the representation in front of him. Men and women of all sizes and shapes, hues and colors clouded his vision. With a slight nudge from his campaign director, Darlene McIntyre, he was cued to begin his speech. In a club that was dominated by white men, he was the minority, and to him, that was a win in and of itself. He had reached the top. A height that no one thought possible. Instead of completing the speech he'd had fully written days prior, he simply shouted, "We did it!"

The crowd erupted in another round of applause as the newly elected senator and his beautiful wife beamed at one another.

Squeezing her hand, as he'd done many times before, he felt Vanessa triumphantly squeeze his back in response. Even if he wanted to say more, he couldn't. The sounds of the supporters were so deafening that Devin could do nothing but wave to the masses. The people wanted nothing more than to celebrate the win of senator-elect, Devin Simmons.

The video concluded and Devin sat back in his chair, smiling, as memories from that night flooded back. The co-hosts of the *Red Table Talk*, three generations of women, stood and clapped, later sharing what that moment meant to them and to people around the nation. Americans from all over were celebrating in his historic victory, and Devin was humbled.

Shifting the conversation, Brenda, Julian and Vanessa joined them at the table and the group discussed an array of topics, including Thaddeus and his illegal activities, plus the recent charges against Regis. Praising the work Vanessa was doing in the community, they briefly shared photos of her in her wedding dress and talked about the birth of baby Reagan.

Affected by addiction in their own family, Brenda was asked to describe her recovery journey. Her sons shared the affect her disease had had on them over the years. At one year sober, Brenda felt better than ever and her boys were thankful that they were able to really get to know her now. Brenda even mentioned that she was dating someone she'd known for years, and smiled. Backstage, Jacob grinned from ear to ear at Brenda's answer. He had been in love with her for years, even throughout her addiction, and was happy she was finally healthy enough to, once again, give love a chance. Devin and Julian approved of their new romance and he was sure Thaddeus did too. Tears were shared, hugs exchanged and the love Devin received during his first interview after getting elected, was unreal. Over a year ago none of them could have ever imagined this moment. The Simmons legacy was back intact and the family was better than ever.

EPILOGUE

Regis should have killed Brittany, but something had prevented him from doing so all those years ago. With so much blood on his hands it was shocking he couldn't take her out, but the truth was, she reminded him of his mother. His mother, who'd birthed him when she was just a kid herself, and had been forced into sex work when she was only twelve years old. Growing up, he remembered the nights when she'd bring men into their one-bedroom apartment, and would do things with them with no regard for Regis or his two sisters. Eventually, his mother was killed by her john, leaving Regis and his sisters to fend for themselves. Seeing Brittany had sparked something in him. It was like he wanted to save her and do for her what he couldn't do for his own mother, but now he regretted it.

Taking his mop and gliding it across the floor, he thought about all his mistakes. As a kid, Regis was certain that choosing a life in politics over the streets was the safest and smartest move. By following Governor Nichols, an older white man who seemed to have the world at his fingertips, as opposed to the gangsters from his neighborhood, he thought he'd have the life he'd always dreamed of. He was well dressed, well-spoken and well educated, yet now he was in the same jail that some of the boys he'd grown up with had passed through on their way to various prisons.

Now, as a senior citizen, it was his turn.

Found guilty on most of the charges against him, Regis was looking at spending the rest of his life in a holding cell. He remained at the Baltimore City Correctional Center, but was scheduled to be shipped off to medium-security prison in Butner, North Carolina by the end of the week. If all he had committed had been white collar crimes he would have gone to a cushy minimum-security prison, or a prison camp, but his crimes were too horrific.

Without any solid evidence or testimony to charge Regis in the murder-for-hire case of Thaddeus, he evaded that charge, but was found guilty of the murder of Congressman Rucker and the attempted murder of Brittany Garcia. Who knew that mirroring the example of a high-powered figure like Governor Nichols would be his downfall and not a gangster like Midnight?

"I never stood a chance in this world," grumbled Regis.

Before he could continue pondering his predicament, a fellow inmate trekked across the hallway, streaking the floor. Opening his mouth to admonish the young man, before he could blink, a blade was plunged into his chest. He was no longer an asset to the Nichols family. Now, he was a liability, and for Brendan, the son of former Governor Gregory Nichols, that meant he had to die. Surrounded by a pool of his own blood, Regis lay motionless next to his mop and bucket, signaling the end of a tumultuous era.

Printed in the USA
CPSIA information can be obtained
at www.ICGtesting.com
LVHW071919180823
755634LV00011B/134